CUT

Persephone has been at home with danger all her life.
One way or another, it's time for her to leave.

LAYLA
HARDING

[PNKHRST]

Also available from Pankhearst

Evangeline Jennings
Riding in Cars with Girls
Extended Play

Simon Paul Wilson
Yuko Zen is Somewhere Else

Slim Volume—Poetry and Flash Fiction
No Love Lost
Wherever You Roam

YA Collections
Heathers
Mermaids
Moremaids

Noir Collection
Cars and Girls

pankhearst.com

CUT

LAYLA
HARDING

[PNKHRST]

As with all things, always and forever, for my daughter

CUT

1.

I started practicing suicide when I was twelve years old. That's kind of funny. It makes it sound like some sort of religion I picked up. She's *a non-practicing Catholic... I'm a practicing suicide.* I guess it was a religion in a way, with its own rituals and services. I was a devout follower.

I always locked my bedroom door. I don't know why. My mother never came to my room, and if my father wanted in, a lock wouldn't stop him. It never did.

Then I chose my music. Something soothing but not too poignant—certainly nothing controversial. It always infuriated me when some kid blew his brains out with Marilyn Manson streaming through Pandora and all of a sudden it's the musician's fault. Marilyn and Ozzy weren't the problem. The demon lurking in the dark didn't bite the heads off live bats or parade around in make-up. He didn't sing. He whispered.

The razors were kept tucked away in the back of a dresser drawer. You know the kind you can buy in a pack of ten for a buck? The kind that will shred your legs if you actually try to shave with them? Other razors would work, but they were damn near impossible to get apart.

Usually I had the plastic casing snapped before the first song was over. I always took such care in the process so I didn't cut my fingers. Don't ask me why—it's like the death row doctor sterilizing the needle for the lethal injection. Another part of the ritual.

The thin blade would glimmer under the lamp next to my bed and sing out the siren song of the depressed. "Use me, trust me. I can make it all better."

I always started with the right arm. I heard in some movie cutting vertically, along the veins, instead of side to side would do more damage. Go up the river, never across. Should someone discover me before I bled out those wounds would be harder to stitch. A Good Samaritan at the ER would have a tough time saving me from me.

After pumping my fist a few times to draw the vein to the surface, I traced its blue line down my arm with the blade. Methodically charting the course before I began my journey. Sometimes my hand shook too much to get it right the first time, so I needed the map.

The first cut followed the path I marked, quick and deep. I was fascinated to see my wrist open up. The layers of skin looked thin and pale like fresh sliced mozzarella. There was a split second when the wound stayed bleach-white as if my body was deciding whether or not it wanted to bleed.

Then there was the big vein itself. It dodged and rolled from side to side, barely avoiding the blade. What would have happened if I ever had severed it? I imagined a geyser of blood spewing out like a scene in a Tarantino movie. It would splash against the furniture and walls, coating everything in a slick, sticky layer of red. When they discovered my lifeless body the next morning, everything would have a warm glow from the sun streaming through the stained glass windows. A cathedral of my own making.

My mother would scream so hard a muscle would rip in her throat, cutting off the shriek prematurely and making her sound like a choking frog. My father would throw up a thin line of brown fluid (the first cup of coffee he drank while reading the paper, wondering why I wasn't out of bed yet). They would try to steady themselves against the walls, realizing too late they were covering themselves with the slick coating of blood on the drywall.

Then the smell would hit them—the rusty, decaying smell of their daughter's body. The entire scene would drive them beyond insanity. Days later, when neither of them had been seen outside of the house, and I had not been in school, the cops would arrive. Poor officers— they wouldn't know what to do with the catatonic couple they found in the basement or the dead girl in the back room. How would they radio it in? This was the part of me that watched too many horror movies.

The other part of me—the part that believed someone still cared— envisioned a scene where my blue-lipped, pale body lay peacefully on the bed. Too weak to save myself I would be Snow White on a crimson bed, my black hair throwing the porcelain of my skin into sharp contrast. I would close my eyes and let go.

In this scene, the discovery was anguished and full of self-blame. How could they not have seen what they were doing to their own daughter? They would yell and berate each other. They would gather my corpse into their arms, hugging and kissing me. They'd beg God to give me back, promising to never make those mistakes again, if He would only give their baby back.

My spirit would watch from above, sad they could not say they were sorry while I was alive but grateful a lesson had been learned. I would reach down and let them know I forgave them. In my own ghostly way, I would tell them to go forth and sin no more. And then I would be free from this world.

But I never could catch the vein. Let's face it—I didn't try too hard. I sat there and watched the blood pool and drip down my arm until it began to slow and clot.

By that time the service was almost over, the final hymn about to be sung. I would pull out the box of bandages from under my bed. It would be long sleeves for me the next few weeks, even in the summer.

At some point it stopped being about suicide, although it was always the goal. The journey, the pain and sacrificing of flesh, began to mean more. The rituals are addictive, like the chills from the first tent revival. People spend their entire lives trying to recapture this simple faith—trying to find the ultimate mountaintop peace. I found a way to wash away my sins with my own blood, but I couldn't find the courage to make it last.

During my senior year I counted a hundred and seventeen scars on my body. They were under my breasts, the inside of my thighs, my hips, lower stomach, and crooks of my elbows. On the nights I needed to control the pain, have a blood rite, I would leave my wrists alone and attack a different part of my body.

What else could I do when the demon lurking in the dark whispered, "Don't worry, honey. It's Daddy," and the only person who wanted to save me was me?

2.

Towards the end of my senior year, I realized it was time to either close the deal or knock off my nasty little habit of slicing myself open. The euphoria still came when I felt the sting of metal on my skin, but I was doing it too often. I looked like a human cutting board, scarred and scored from overuse.

I came to this conclusion the morning after a particularly brutal session. As usual I struggled to figure out what to wear. Mom said it was supposed to be hot. Without missing a beat, I explained with the new air conditioning system in the school, it got downright cold in there.

I liked keeping track of the lies I told during the day. I put them in little columns in my head: lies I told that people believed; lies people believed because it made their lives easier; and lies no one in their right mind should ever believe but they didn't care enough to call me out on. I never needed a column for lies people called BS on.

One of the cuts from the night before opened up while I was pulling my hair back. I had sliced deeper than I'd thought. If I'd had more courage I wouldn't have been getting ready at all.

The mountaintop feeling was quickly replaced by guilt. When the blood started rolling down my arm I felt dirty. I wanted to get back in the shower and scrub my body raw. I never felt nastier than the day after cutting. The line of blood was a billboard advertising my failure. I couldn't end it, but I couldn't stop trying. I never did drugs (not even a joint), but I could imagine what the crash felt like. It sucked.

On the way to school I smoked like a fiend. Some people (hateful, rotten people who couldn't mind their own business) told me I was slowly killing myself with this disgusting habit. That was the whole point. Idiots. I hated when people felt the need to comment on things they knew nothing about.

Pulling my backpack from the car, I banged my wrist. I waited a few minutes to make sure it wasn't going to open up. *This is going to be a long damn day.*

And I was right. It was filled with the mundane minutiae of normality. Meaningless conversations in the hallways, teachers intent on shaping young minds into their agendas, and an inedible lunch. I told my English teacher my hard drive crashed and promised to turn in my homework the next day. The paper was actually safely tucked away in my bag—I just wanted to see if she would let me get away with it. She did. I told the girl sitting next to me in Calculus her Lucky jeans so did not make her butt look fat—if anything they made it look smaller. I didn't say I meant compared to a rhino's ass. And I told the football player who asked me out he was way too good for me and going out with him would only make me nervous. The only thing that made me nervous was the thought of an entire night watching him struggle to carry on a coherent conversation that didn't involve first downs. It was amazing the shit people would buy to preserve their sense of balance in the world.

The only abnormal part of my day was the constant vibration of my cell phone. There were four calls from a number I didn't recognize. On the last one whoever it was finally left a voicemail. I was mildly curious to see who they thought they were calling but had to wait until the end of school to check. The penalties for on-campus cell phone use were harsh.

Because I sat on the fringe of the popular crowd, I could go unnoticed for days if I kept my head down. My family was upper-middle class and that was the best way to describe my social status. I knew about all the parties, but no one would ever miss me if I wasn't there. I would never be on the Homecoming court, but I would always have a date to the dance. When I wanted friends, I could find them. When I didn't, no one came looking for me. I rarely wanted friends.

I think I was only ever included out of a vague sense of guilt and a high schooler's need to keep the world making sense. I came from a semi-wealthy family. I was pretty (not traffic-stopping or anything, but pretty). I was in the top ten of my class. I was supposed to want to belong. I was supposed to want to be a part of 'them'. As long as they felt I was still there somewhere, close by, all was right with the world. The cliques were in place, the social structure unshaken, and rose-colored glasses remained firmly attached to faces.

After my last class, I raced through the halls and out to my car. Two blocks from school, I could light a much needed cigarette. It cracked me up. The security officer could smell a smoke you had two days ago and bust you for it. On the other hand, he couldn't seem to catch the kids popping Oxy and Vicodin in the bathrooms at lunch. All a matter of priorities I guess.

I had barely taken the first drag when my phone lit up again.

"Hello?"

"Um yes. I was tryin' to reach Ken Austin."

"Wrong number."

"Are you sure?"

"I think I know my own number."

"Sorry to trouble you, miss."

I deleted the voicemail without listening to it.

Later that night I sat in my room staring at my Calculus book, listening to my parents' footsteps above me. Mom's slowed as the night progressed (it was hard to walk after a gallon of gin and tonics). Dad's sped up as he paced from his office to the bathroom to the kitchen.

He didn't like being at home and walked around the house with the frustration of a caged hyena. I knew why he preferred being on the road, but I wasn't sure who she was. It was either the chick from Human Resources who somehow ended up on a lot of his sales trips or his assistant. They both had the look of professional gold diggers, and either way, he got cranky when he was home for too long.

When it seemed his pacing had finally ceased (where he ended up was anyone's guess—God knows it wasn't in Mom's room. They hadn't shared a bed since I was a little girl), I gave up on the pages of equations in front of me. I had been staring at the same problem for almost thirty minutes, and it still wasn't any clearer than when I began.

My piano called from the room across the hall. A few songs and I would get back to work. Music's supposed to be good for your brain, right? Aren't you supposed to listen to classical music when doing math? Could I rationalize abandoning my homework? Of course I could.

Sitting down in front of the keys, I felt my shoulders relax and the knots start to loosen in my back. Music was my one pure escape. It had never been touched or tainted by anything bad. Well, there was that one time, right after my first little brush with a razor blade. My piano teacher noticed the cuts and asked me what had happened. I made up some lame excuse about losing a fight with my cat—I didn't own a cat. It was also my first experience with lies people believe to make their lives easier. It was shocking and invigorating.

After the lesson, I told my mom pursuing a music career probably wasn't in the cards for me. I wanted to keep playing as a hobby, but I didn't need lessons anymore. She acquiesced without a fight. I think she was happy not to drive forty minutes each way four times a week.

That aside, everything about playing was wonderful. Mom purchased the piano for me as a Christmas present shortly after I began playing. It was a second-hand Steinway but in perfect condition. I fell in love the moment I saw it.

The piano started out in the downstairs living room. After one night too many playing after ten, my mom decided I needed a music room. Two weeks later the subcontractors soundproofed the bedroom across from mine. Mom picked out a rich, thick beige carpet, two overstuffed leather chairs and a matching coffee table even though I was the only person who would ever be in there. Every inch of the room was perfect, and it was the best present Mom ever gave me.

Sometimes I would sit in my room for hours, playing whatever came into my head, playing until my fingers ached and refused to stretch across the keys anymore. I could tell from the moment I hit the first note it was going to be one of those nights.

My phone lit up three more times with the same unknown number while I was playing. Part of me thought about calling the guy back, let him know he was getting the wrong number—*still*—but I decided not to. Surely he would figure it out on his own. Or he would keep calling me. It wasn't my job to help out some dumbass who couldn't figure out how to dial a phone correctly.

3.

Friday night was party night. I wasn't particularly excited about going out, but I promised my friend, Maggie, I would, and well, it was something to do. It was better than being at home, and Maggie was the only person in my life I wanted around on a semi-regular basis.

"So what's the deal with the idiot they're passing off as an English teacher?" she asked, lighting a cigarette.

"Did you do the 'who am I' project?" We were introduced to our new English teacher at mid-semester—a replacement for the less than moral Mr Forrester who had a thing for his prettier students. The rumor was he picked the wrong student this time and impregnated her. We all had our theories about who the lucky recipient of the dangling participle was.

Forrester's replacement was a freshly scrubbed, peppy little thing named Ms Hall. The kindest thing I could say about her was she reminded me of an After School special. Her latest assignment was to come up with a poem, collage, or essay to explain who we thought we "really" were. There were only two important things about us—we were desperate to graduate and equally desperate to get accepted into colleges as far away from our parents as possible. How do you turn that into a collage?

"Yeah, I made a photocopy of that stupid poster with the kitten on it. You know the one that says 'hang in there'? Then I put balloons and hearts all over it."

I almost choked, inhaling. "Are you kidding me? That's hilarious!" Maggie puffed up, pleased with her cleverness.

As much as we were alike in our personalities, Maggie and I were at opposite ends of the spectrum when it came to appearances. I had inherited my father's height, but thankfully not his girth. Maggie was lucky to stretch to a full five feet. Whereas my hair was long, curly and dark, hers was cropped close to her head and almost white blonde. Maggie joked if we were road signs I would be Dangerous Curves Ahead, and she would be Slow Children at Play.

"I was going to make it all dark and black to flip her out, but I figured there were enough douche bags doing that, being serious, thinking they were being all non-conformist and shit. It probably freaks her out more to think there's a happy, optimistic kid in the class."

"That's classic. Can't wait to see what you get on it."

"What did you do?"

"Oh, this stupid little poem thing. Nothing major. She's the type to give an A because you turned something in. I didn't put a lot of time into it."

It was true. With everything that had happened the night before the assignment was due, I barely spent ten minutes throwing some words together on a piece of notebook paper.

Dad was home that night. When I got back from whatever it was I did to stay away as long as possible, Mom had already passed out. To be fair, it was after nine—long past her evening sober window. The minute I walked in the door, he ended his call. I wondered which one of the chippies he was talking to.

He ran his hand over his completely bald head, a nervous habit. It was a holdover from the days when he still had hair, which was when I was an infant. Mom said he began losing it in his early twenties. Instead of fighting it, he shaved it all off.

When I was little I loved the stubbly feel when he didn't take the time to shave on the weekends. I would run my hands over his head, tickling my own palms and laughing wildly. Then we would run through the house, me squealing and him growling. When he finally caught me he would nuzzle the underside of my chin with his stubble. I would shriek louder and louder until Mom would finally holler for both of us to quiet down. In those moments he was my Daddy, and I loved him.

"Where the hell have you been?" His tone was full of fake indignation. He knew as my father he should have been worried I was out after dark and hadn't called to let him know my whereabouts. The truth was he probably hadn't realized I was gone until I appeared at the front door.

"Out. I didn't think you were home. You were supposed to be on a trip."

"It got cancelled, and that's no excuse. You should have called."

"Sorry. I need to go do my homework."

"Persephone, this is not a hotel. You cannot just come and go as you please." *Pot meet kettle.* "You may think you're all grown up, but you're still living under our roof. There are rules. It is downright

inconsiderate to make your mother and me worry about you like this."
Dear God, why did his trip have to get cancelled? With Mom
incapacitated I was the one who had to deal with his foul humor. He
was really going to try to do the whole parenting thing. I just wanted
to get away.

"I said I was sorry. It won't happen again. Dad, seriously. I have a
lot of homework to do."

"Whatever."

I should have known it wouldn't end there. He needed something
to keep himself entertained if he was going to be stuck at the house. I
was only in the shower for a few minutes when I heard the bathroom
door open. I could see his silhouette through the shower curtain—
which meant he could see mine.

"I thought you said you had homework to do, Persephone." *Get
out, get out, get out,* my brain screamed.

"I do, but I needed a shower."

"Why? What have you been doing?" *Go away!*

"I can't hear you over the water, Dad!"

"Then turn it off and get out here."

"Soap in my hair! Be out in a moment!"

His hand slithered in and shut off the water. "Now, Persephone."
He pulled the curtain back and handed me a towel. I snatched it, hiding
my body as quickly as I could. The brief glimpse was enough.
Satisfaction flickered in his eyes. He could make me do whatever he
wanted, no matter how old I was.

"Go do your homework." And he walked out.

Homework was put on hold while I carved a pattern of hash marks
across my left hip. One for the first time he touched me. Another for
the first time Mom got drunk. A third for the first time I realized there

was nothing I could do about either. And one last cut for the first time I didn't cry because there were no tears left.

"Persephone, are you okay to drive? I'm ready to go." Maggie was at my arm, eyes a little red, speech a whole lot slurred. Thankfully, I saw where the night was going within thirty minutes of arriving and drank accordingly. Maggie was obviously not going to exhibit a lot of self-control. It was amazing how much Red Bull and vodka a girl her size could put away before ten o'clock.

"Yeah, I'm good. Let's get out of here." We half-heartedly mumbled our goodbyes. A few idiots whined the party was just getting started. I saw some plastic baggies peeking out of jacket pockets and knew I wanted no part of the next phase of the night.

"You want to stay over? Dad's on a trip, so it's only Mom at the house."

"Yeah, that's sounds good." Maggie's head lolled on the headrest.

"Hey, Maggie, do you think God exists?"

"Sure, and He hates me."

"No, seriously. Do you believe in God?"

"Yeah, I guess so. I mean, how could you not? There has to be some ultimate power creator-type force out there. But do I believe in the whole Jesus loves me crap? C'mon. Have you looked at our parents recently?"

What could I say? She had a point and she was too drunk to debate the issue further.

After tucking her in, I sat on my floor thinking about what Maggie said. Little strains of Bible school songs played in my head. *Jesus loves me, this I know, for the Bible tells me so... This little light of mine, I'm gonna let it shine... Jesus loves the little children... Suffer the little children, come unto Me.* And then my phone rang. It was the same number as before. Who the hell called someone this late at night? I was fed up.

"Hello?" Silence. *"Hello?"*

"Um, yes, is Ken there?"

"No, Ken is not here. As a matter of fact, you will never reach Ken at this number no matter how many times you call it because this is *not* Ken's phone! This is *my* phone! And I would appreciate it if you told Ken the next time you actually call him instead of me to *stop giving my number out!*"

"I'm so sorry, miss. I guess this isn't 555-8786?"

"No! This is 555-8687." *What a moron.*

"I do apologize, miss. Ken's an old buddy and not doin' too well. Guess I musta misdialed. I won't bother you again. You have a good night now."

Wow, did I feel like the biggest bitch on the planet. Poor guy was only checking on his friend, got the numbers confused, and I went off on him. *Nice going, Persephone. Maybe tomorrow you can go kick some puppies.*

4.

Maggie's mom called at some God-awful hour the next morning, demanding her daughter's immediate presence at home. That meant I had to drag myself out of bed and drive her there. On the way back home, I started thinking about the poor guy on the other end of my tirade the night before. I actually worked up a pretty high level of guilt about my behavior. It wasn't his fault my life sucked. My need to make it right was overwhelming, as weird as that was. I pulled my phone out and scrolled through the recent calls. There it was—multiple times. I pushed call.

"Ken?" His voice was anxious. Apparently he still didn't have Ken's correct number programmed into his phone.

"No, sir. This is the girl you called last night by accident." Total silence. He was probably scared I was going to start ranting again. "Um, I wanted to say I was sorry. You didn't deserve to be yelled at. It was an honest mistake, and I took a lot of personal frustration out on you." It was a pretty truthful explanation. I felt the need to throw in some really wild lie to make up for my honesty, but he didn't give me the chance.

"Well, that's awful nice of you. Not too many people would do that. Ken and I were in the Marines together years ago, and he's been kinda under the weather lately. I try to keep in touch—make sure he's still hangin' in there." The guy had a southern lilt to his voice that made the end of his words disappear. It was kind of charming.

This was the perfect opportunity for me to lie. I could have told him my grandfather was in the Marines, too. Or that my father was sick and dying (I wished). The truth was my grandfather had been a con man at best and died when I was thirteen. My grandmother followed him to the grave shortly thereafter. She actually loved the son of a bitch and most people said she died of a broken heart. And, of course, my father was in perfect health.

I don't know what kept me from telling him any one of the innocuous white lies flying through my head. It wasn't like I was ever going to meet the man. What would it matter? I told bigger lies to people I saw every day. Instead I heard myself saying, "I'm sorry to hear that. Have you gotten a hold of him yet?"

"No, miss, I haven't. I'm startin' to get a little worried about him. Course, I'm not sure I've dialed his actual number more'n a couple of times." There was a little chuckle. "I live up here in Kansas City, so I can't really pop over and see him."

"Well, maybe I could check on him for you. It's not like Springfield's a real big town. It wouldn't be hard." What the hell? Where had that come from? Not lying to the man was one thing, but I never offered to do anything I didn't want to. I wasn't that nice—as my grandmother was kind enough to point out in her final days.

About a week before she died, she was put in the hospital. Somehow, one evening, I ended up in the room alone with her. She took my hand and asked, "Who are you, Persephone? Why are you so mean and deceitful? You used to be such a sweet child." My mouth hung open. I wanted to slap the shit out of her. "It was right after your sixth birthday. It was almost like you fell asleep one night, and a little monster woke up in your place."

Nice words from a grandmother, huh? I felt like telling her she was absolutely correct. Right after my sixth birthday was when my father "visited" my room for the first time. A different kid *did* wake up the next day—a kid that felt like telling her grandma to burn in hell.

Instead, I kissed her cheek, walked out and never went back. She died three days later. I didn't shed a single tear at the funeral.

"No, no, no. He's a tough old bird, and I'm sure he's doin' fine." Whew, dodged a bullet on that one. "'Sides, I don't know that he'd answer the door to a stranger. Then again, the way things are goin' everyone might be a stranger to him soon." He laughed at his own joke, but it sounded hollow. He was worried about his friend and trying to make the best of the situation.

"Okay, well, if you change your mind, I guess you have my number."

He chuckled again. "That I do, miss, that I do. Thanks again for callin'."

Since Maggie was tied up the rest of the day with her mother, I had to find ways to avoid my own maternal figure. Holing up in the piano room seemed like the most viable option. I rifled through sheet music trying to find something to fit my mood. One of the biggest problems with playing was when I couldn't find the right song, I ended up more frustrated and angst-ridden. It was worse than coming home starving and finding nothing you wanted in the pantry or fridge.

This appeared to be one of those mornings. I could feel my mood darkening and the rage escalating the longer I sat with my fingers drifting over the keys, stabbing random notes. So what the hell was I going to do now? Boredom and anger were a deadly combination for a teenager with an affinity for razors. But I didn't like to cut when the sun was up—a quirk of mine, I guess.

I hated coffee shops—pseudo-intellectuals pretending to have meaningful conversations. Sitting in the park would require me bearing witness to actual happy families. That pretty much left driving around aimlessly, smoking, and flipping through crappy radio stations.

The thing about Springfield was when you needed to get somewhere traffic would ensure a mile took thirty minutes. When you had nowhere to go, you could drive the entire city in fifteen minutes or less. On my second trip through the same intersection, my phone started buzzing. It was Ken's friend.

"Hello?" I answered, expecting him to be embarrassed he had misdialed again.

"Uh, hello. This is the man that accidentally keeps callin' you."

"Uh huh?"

"Well, I feel kinda silly askin' you this, but I finally got a hold of Ken. He doesn't have much family to speak of, and he likes to read." I couldn't figure out what one had to do with the other or why either one had anything to do with me. "I was wonderin' if you really meant what you said about goin' to check on him?"

"I guess so." Me and my stupid mouth. I meant it at the time. Now, not so much.

"It's okay if you were just bein' polite. I mean, I know we're complete strangers. I don't even know your name now that I think about it."

"It's Persephone."

"Well, Miss Persephone, my name is James Fry."

"Nice to meet you, Mr Fry. So to speak." I was trying to find the happy line between polite and disconnected. Perhaps a chilly tone would head off wherever this was going. On the other hand, I hated to be rude to him again. I was pretty sure I already banked enough bad karma for one week.

"You too, miss. Here's my predicament. Like I said, Ken likes to read, but his eyesight isn't real good anymore. He keeps losing track of where he is, getting headaches, that kinda thing. Old age ain't much fun."

"I would imagine not." *Well, there was a profound insight, Persephone.*

"I don't suppose you would be willin' to go over there and read to him a bit, would you?" He sounded so hopeful I couldn't say no, even though I had no idea what I was getting myself into. These guys could be scam artists who lured young girls into a prostitution ring for all I knew. What a delightful turn of events that would be.

Now, instead of a horror movie playing out my death, I saw a poignant drama—a Lifetime movie. I would go missing, posters would be plastered all over the town, and my parents would appear on the news pleading for someone, anyone to come forward. Please tell us where our baby is, kind of thing.

Months later, my body would be found in the woods, malnourished, abused, and abandoned. I could see myself wrapped in a huge tarp, a horrible Christmas present left behind for an unsuspecting hunter to find and open. I only needed the courage to show up at the guy's house. Fate could take over from there.

"Sure, not a problem. What's his address?" Now that I had warmed to the idea and all its glorious possibilities, I wanted to get over there as soon as possible.

"He lives on Buena Vista, southwest side of town. I've been there a couple of times, so I could probably give you directions."

"No, I know where that is. It's only a couple of streets north of mine, and I have GPS. I'm free today if you want me to go over."

"I'm sure he would like that. I should probably call, let him know. Are you sure you want to do this? I hadn't told him I might have someone, so it's not like you would be disappointin' him. I'm thinkin' from the sound of your voice, you can't be more'n sixteen. Surely you have better things to do than read to some cranky old Marine."

Like what? Stare at my bedroom walls trying to talk myself out of cutting another part of my body? Pray that when Dad came home from his next trip I got at least one good night's sleep? No thank you.

"No, I'm good." *And if you could convince your friend to take care of this pesky little being alive problem I have that would be great.*

"Course, I'll pay you for your time."

"That won't be necessary. You can tell Ken I'll be there around two or so. Will that work?"

"Yes, ma'am. I just can't thank you enough for this. It means the world to me and will mean even more to him."

That afternoon I sat in Ken's driveway wondering what in the hell I was thinking when I agreed to this. Nothing like having second thoughts after it was too late in the game. It was kind of like regretting sex after the STD test came back positive. You pretty much had to take your medicine and hope for the best.

A quarter mile and a different way of life separated my neighborhood from Ken's. The houses were nothing to be ashamed of but would definitely never make Better Homes magazine. They were about what you would expect for a newly married couple or retiree. I sat as long as I could and decided it was time to stop staring and go meet the man within. Heaven help me.

When Mary Shelley described Frankenstein's monster, I can only imagine she knew there would one day be a man like Ken Austin. At a little over five feet nine inches, I was by no means petite. This guy made me feel like a hobbit. His shoulders could have borne the weight of a small country and his hands could have held another two. His hair was kept in the same military cut from his youth, which showed every odd bump and roll of his skull. Could a brain even function in a head shaped like that?

But it was his eyes that caused me to squeak instead of belting out the clear, commanding introduction I practiced the whole way over. Imagine a pristine, crystal blue pond. Now add a layer of ice. That's what was staring at me from the doorway. In his younger days, I'm sure those eyes made every female between the ages of ten and one hundred fall in love. Now they scared the shit out of me.

"Um, Mr Austin... um, I..."

"Are you Persephone? I thought you would be older." His voice matched his appearance in every way. It rumbled out of his chest like a sonic boom and vibrated in my stomach. It took all my self-control not to run at a full sprint away from the house. "Well, come in."

His home was exactly as I suspected—orderly and uncluttered as a Marine barracks. I was pretty sure I would find hospital corners on his bed and everything hung neatly by color in his closet.

Despite the neatness, there was a faint smell under it. It was almost imperceptible if you didn't know it should be there. Sickness was circling this house like a plane in a holding pattern at LAX on a holiday weekend. No one knew when it was going to be cleared for landing, but it was only a matter of time.

"James said you could read."

"Yes, sir."

"I hope you read louder than you talk."

I cleared my throat. "Yes, sir."

"That's better. How old are you?"

"Seventeen."

"You're just a pup, aren't you?"

"Yes, sir."

"The living room is this way."

There was a recliner, rocking chair, and three floor to ceiling bookshelves. I could see why he didn't have many visitors. Where in the hell would they sit? Which chair was meant for me? Ken settled himself into the overstuffed recliner, leaving the massive oak rocking chair. My butt would be numb in ten minutes.

"How do you feel about John Irving?" I knew the name—kind of. I mean, who hasn't heard about John Lithgow's famous cross-dressing role? As for reading any of his books—yeah, well, reading wasn't really my thing.

"He's fine? I mean, I've never really read anything by him, but that's okay."

"It's time to broaden your horizons then. There aren't any vampires or werewolves, but maybe you can struggle through somehow."

Wow, did I get my nose thumped? Was this guy actually condescending to me? Seriously, I was the one doing him the favor. Besides I never watched a single movie in that whole ridiculous series, much less picked up one of the books. Even someone like me had her standards. As I opened my mouth to say as much, it dawned on me that every Chuck Norris fact could apply to the man in front of me. My death wish was in sudden conflict with my basic instinct to not get the shit beaten out of me. I closed my mouth.

"The book is beside you on the floor."

I hefted the novel onto my lap. How many hours did he think I was going to be here? I flipped past the table of contents and dedication page. "Okay, so, *A Prayer for Owen Meany* by John Irving. The Foul Ball."

It didn't take long, the first sentence really, ("I was doomed to remember a boy with a wrecked voice") for me to be intrigued. I had never read anything even close to this kind of book, and I was surprised by how much I liked it. I completely lost track of time until I heard a sharp snore and was startled out of the story.

Closing the book, I looked around the room. There were a few pictures on the bookshelves. One was of Ken a long time ago, standing next to a striking man, both in full Marine dress. I wondered if the other man was James.

Right beside it was one of Ken, a slightly younger version, standing next to a girl. She barely came up to his chest. Just as she stared adoringly at him, he was returning her gaze with full force. Girlfriend?

Sister? Whoever she was, where the hell was she? Why wasn't she here putting up with him instead of me?

If Ken hadn't been quite so big, or if I had been sure of how soundly he slept, I would have wandered through the rest of the house. Instead, I took one more look around and spotted a fleece blanket on the floor next to his recliner. Quietly, I picked it up and shook it out. Sure enough, the Marine emblem was printed on the middle. After covering him up, I let myself out.

5.

My phone started chirping on the way to school Monday morning. It was James.

"Hello?"

"Good mornin', Miss Persephone. Hope I'm not disturbin' you."

"Nope, just on my way to school. What can I do for you?" It was more polite than my regular 'what do you want' but not by much. Honestly, I didn't have the energy to be nice at that moment. As a matter of fact, I rarely had the energy to be nice. I needed all of my strength to maintain.

"Well, I wanted to let you know Ken called me last night. You make quite a first impression, young lady." Oh shit, what had I done? Great, now I was going to have two pissed off Marines plotting against me. Just what I needed to make my life complete. On the other hand, there could be advantages.

"I'm sorry?"

"No apologies needed, miss. I guess that was a bad way of sayin' that. Ken was actually quite taken with you. Said you even took the

29

time to cover him up before you left. That was real sweet." *Taken with me?* Yeah, right. Whatever human emotion (other than disdain) that man possessed was used up on the woman in the photo.

"I didn't know what else to do."

"Heard he has you reading that boring ole John Irving. One of his favorites. Tried to make me read it years ago. Sorry about that."

"I think I'll be okay. Does he want me to come back over?" I wasn't entirely sure if I wanted him to say yes or no.

"Yes, he would like that very much, but I don't want to take advantage of you, Persephone. I'm sure you have friends you'd much rather be with than takin' care of him."

"No, that's alright. I don't mind. Maybe Wednesday after school? About four-thirty?"

"I'm sure that'd be just fine. By the way, how'd he look to you?" I told James his friend looked good. *Liar, liar, pants on fire.*

"Good to hear. I know he says he's doin' alright, but it's not the same as seein' it myself."

"Totally understand. I guess I could call you when I get done Wednesday if you want."

"That'd be great, if you don't mind it too much. By the by, if you want to, Ken loves peanut butter cups. It would probably make him happy to get some. Marines never stop being Marines, you know. He may be a little gruff, but he's a good man."

Whatever. It must be nice to have a built-in excuse for being an asshole. But if it meant he might actually smile, I guess I was willing to give it a try.

"Thanks, I'll keep that in mind."

"Guess that's that then. Thank you, Persephone. This is a wonderful thing you're doin'."

Wednesday I made time to stop by a gas station and pick up several packs of peanut butter cups and a huge Diet Coke. Maggie called while I was paying, but I didn't answer. If it was really important she would text.

Ken opened the door after the second knock.

"So you decided to come back?" It was hard to tell if he was pissed or pleased.

"Yes, sir."

"Come in then. No point in standing in the doorway staring at each other." I stepped around him as he pulled the door shut. "Do you want something to drink? I have water and unsweet tea. Don't understand the sweet stuff. James always tries to tell me it's the only way to drink it. Southerns." He snorted. "Tastes like liquid sugar if you ask me. Makes my teeth hurt." It was damn near an oratory compared to how much he had spoken the first time.

"No thanks. I brought something to drink. And, um, I brought you these." I held out the paper bag full of candy. "James said you like them."

"Is that so?" He peered into the bag, and I thought I saw the corners of his mouth twitch. Was that his version of a smile? If so, it needed work.

"Alright then. You go on in. I'm going to get a glass of water." *Um, a thank you would be nice.* Oh well. It wasn't like I expected much more from anyone else in my life.

"Yes, sir." And I was definitely using that word way too much, but I couldn't help it. The man didn't only command respect—he reached out and snatched it from you.

The living room hadn't changed in the past few days, except there was now a small pillow on the seat of the rocking chair. Wow, was he actually trying to make me more comfortable?

"You going to sit down?" Ken was at my shoulder, with his glass of water. He startled me so badly, I almost knocked it out of his hand and onto the floor.

"Oh shit! Sorry! I mean, yes, sir." Good Lord, could I be any more of a dork? And did I really cuss in front of him? So much for the sweet little high school girl sacrificing her time to read to an old man.

He didn't say anything, but nodded towards the empty chair. Great, I'd offended him. It was pretty obvious he wasn't some crazy serial killer. He wasn't going to do me the favor of ending my life, but it wasn't exactly horrible going over there.

Three pages into reading, I heard the rustle of the paper bag and cellophane wrapper of the peanut butter cups. I glanced up in time to see him pop one whole into his mouth. The weird little twitch of his lips happened again. Two almost-smiles in one day. How special.

It took about an hour and an entire Big Gulp for Ken to drift off. His breathing slowed and settled into a deep rhythm—my signal to stop for the day. The blanket was in the same place as before, so I covered him up and tiptoed to the front door. On the entryway table was an envelope with my name scrawled across it. Inside were two crisp ten dollar bills.

I told James I didn't need to be paid. Had he not told Ken? Did Ken not listen? It didn't matter. Twenty dollars was a month's worth of gas money. It meant a month of not having to ask Dad for anything. How could I not take it?

On the way home, I called James.

"Hello, Miss Persephone. How we doin' this evening?"

"Pretty good. Ken's asleep."

"Good. I'm sure he needs the rest. Are you goin' over there again soon?"

"We didn't really talk about it. I mean, like I said, he was asleep when I left. I could probably go back over on Saturday. Sometime in the afternoon?"

"I'm sure he would like that. Just show up whenever. I don't think his social calendar is too booked."

"Alright. I guess I'll call you Saturday then."

"Sounds great, Persephone. You have a good night, and God bless."

God bless me. Now wouldn't that be a nice change of pace?

With Dad not due home for a few more days, my evening was quiet. Mom was out by ten, and I wrapped up my homework even earlier. I put my phone on silent because Maggie wouldn't stop texting, sat down at my piano, and played until my fingers refused to move. I realized as I got into bed that every piece I played was almost happy, and I hadn't thought about cutting once. Sleep was almost immediate and peaceful.

6.

"So where did you disappear to yesterday?" Maggie leaned against her car, fiddling with her keys. We were a block from school, enjoying one last cigarette together before heading home.

"Oh, just some errands." There was no good reason for not telling Maggie the truth except I hadn't lied to her (or anyone else for that matter) in almost twelve hours.

"So what are you doing tonight? Your dad in town?"

"Yeah, trip got cut short. Mom texted me earlier. Guess he got home sometime this afternoon. Want to do something?" It was comforting that Maggie didn't need an explanation. She accepted that I avoided the house whenever he was there.

"Sure. Mom's going out with the newest one tonight, so we should have the house to ourselves. You can spend the night if you want." Maggie's mom was single and seemed hell-bent on dating every male over the age of twenty-five in the county.

"Where'd she get this one?"

"Dublin's Pass, two nights ago. Seriously, how many love stories have you heard begin with 'we met in a bar'? It's pathetic."

"I'm sorry, man. Do you ever wonder why they even had us? Really. It's obvious they don't like being parents. I mean when was the last time either one of us saw our mothers sober?"

Maggie and I spent many an hour bitching about our mothers' shared pastime. While my mother sequestered herself in a bedroom with any alcohol she could get her hands on, Maggie's mom enjoyed being on display when she was intoxicated. .

A few times I had gotten close to telling Maggie the whole story— why I didn't want to ever be at home, why I hated my father so much. But what if she told her mom? Or heaven forbid, someone with real authority? No one would believe me. My father would deny it. My mother would finally go over the edge she had been teetering on for years. Besides, it was one thing when a little girl was messed with, but a teenager? Would Maggie look at me different? God, the possibilities made me feel light-headed.

It was better to keep lying. Maybe, if I lied enough, I would start to believe it. Like the scars I hid beneath long sleeves, I tucked these truths away. If no one could see them, maybe I could convince myself they didn't really exist.

The silence stretched out. Finally, Maggie spoke.

"You hungry?" Food—Maggie's cure for everything. She was one of those horrible, annoying people that could eat her weight in Oreos then have the nerve to complain she couldn't seem to gain weight. If I didn't love her so much, I would have hated her with every ounce of my soul.

"Yeah, sure. Sushi?"

We took separate cars to our favorite sushi bar, giving me way too much time in my own head. Time to think about the nights Maggie's house wasn't an option. The nights I lay awake waiting for my bedroom door to sigh open, his figure filling the space, wearing nothing but his blue terrycloth robe. Or the nights, exhausted, I would finally fall asleep, only to feel his fingers slide along the sole of my foot, jerking me awake. The small touches, the stink of his breath on my neck, the coldness in his eyes... in those dark hours I was not his daughter. I wasn't even a person. I was a toy. All I could think was *What a bastard.*

When I returned home the next evening, I was pleasantly surprised to find my father's car absent from the driveway. Mom was puttering around in the kitchen, half-heartedly pulling out the ingredients for a dinner for two.

"Hey, Persephone, how was school today? Did you have fun at Maggie's?"

"Good and yes. Where's Dad? Thought he was back for a few days since his trip got cut short."

"So did I. Apparently, there was some crisis at the new restaurant in Dallas. He felt he should attend to it personally." I wondered what her name was. "He left this morning."

"Oh." What a slice of pleasantness—an unexpected night of peace. As long as I could keep the nightmares at bay. "So what's for dinner?"

"Nothing major. I was thinking about chicken casserole. Or maybe I'll order pizza. What do you think?"

"Pizza sounds good."

"Okay." We both stood there, me staring at her, Mom staring at the countertop.

"Mom, is something wrong?"

"Huh? Oh no, just kind of spaced out there for a minute. Sorry, hon. Pepperoni good?"

"Yeah, sounds great. Are you sure you're okay?"

"I'm fine, baby," she answered, still gazing at the counter, as if talking to it instead of me. "Persephone, you would tell me if there was something wrong, right?" She raised her eyes to meet mine. I broke eye contact. Where was this coming from?

"Yeah, Mom. Why?"

"It's just sometimes... I don't know. You seem so distant, I guess."

I tried to laugh it off. "I'm a teenager. That's my job, right?"

"That's what your dad said too, but it's more than that."

Of course that's what Dad said. He must have seen the same thing in her eyes. She didn't know what she was dangerously close to, but her instinct was telling her there was something wrong. I couldn't believe she didn't know. There were times I could almost taste the wrongness in my house. Surely Mom could, too.

If only one of us could have been brave enough to throw the first rock, break through the glass walls surrounding us. They enclosed the members of my little family. And what wonderful walls of funhouse glass they were. Looking out at the world through them, everything was distorted and ugly. But to those looking in, they saw the perfection of a successful, all-American family. We were a display at a museum. We were something to be admired but never touched. Don't get too close—it's against the rules.

We both kept our silence that night. I continued to look at my hands while Mom waited for something to happen. Then she shook her head like a dog waking up from a nap.

"Well, go get your homework done, then. I'll holler at you when the pizza gets here."

On my way down the stairs I heard the rattle of the cabinet as she took down a wine glass. I went to find the sheet music for "On My Own" from *Les Mis*.

7.

Saturday morning I stumbled out of bed long before I was normally up and around. Maggie and I had made our usual round of parties the night before, but I called it quits early on. Maggie hadn't been much in the mood for drinking, so I didn't have to worry about her making it home safe and sound. She had been kind of morose, grunting in response to my questions, barely smiling at all. I wasn't in the mood and didn't have the energy to deal with it.

Mom was cratered when I got home and comatose in the morning. I put on a pot of coffee and threw some cinnamon rolls in the oven. Either the smells would entice her out of bed or they wouldn't. I tried to care one way or the other but couldn't muster it.

On one hand, I was furious with myself for not spilling it all when I had the chance. On the other hand, why the hell did she even need to ask? She was my mother, for God's sake. How could she not know something was wrong? Something was horribly wrong. Seriously. Maybe if she'd stopped living in a Stoli bottle she would have had a clue what was going on in her house.

There were times in my childhood when it seemed Mom realized what she was doing to herself and, by extension, me. She even went so far as to buy one of those love yourself, I'm okay, you're okay books to help with her drinking.

Two days later, Dad laid into her about something. He did it so often I don't even remember what it was about. Eventually the argument degenerated into the name-calling and accusing phase. When Mom questioned him about something, he responded with, "You see, that's why Persephone can't stand being around you. You nag her as badly as you do me. I understand you can't get being a wife right, but you could at least try to be a decent mother."

And there it was—his fallback position. He told me for as long as I could remember that the best defense was a good offense, and he definitely practiced what he preached. It was Mom's weakness, her meltdown button—questioning her skills as a mother and her relationship with me. All else was forgotten as she curled inside herself. As Dad convinced her over and over that she was failing me, her guilt and pain consumed her.

The next day the book was used as a coaster for her cocktail glass. It is difficult to maintain your resolve when the harsh light of reality comes busting through. How many times had I promised myself I would never cut again, only to scramble for a razor later that same day? You do what you need to survive. Mom had to drink her way through a hellish marriage. I cut my way through our hellish family. Booze or blood, there was no real difference. We were dealing with our pain.

As the rolls were coming out of the oven, Mom shuffled in. "Good morning, sweetheart. I didn't hear you come in last night. Did you have fun?"

You wouldn't have heard a Cat-5 hurricane last night. "Yeah, we had a good time. Actually, I got home kind of early. You were already asleep."

"Oh, I must have been really tired." *Whatever.* "You have any big plans today?"

"Oh, this and that. Have some errands to run later this afternoon."

"Well that sounds nice. I think I will be lazy today. Maybe play in the garden a little. Will you be home for dinner?"

"I can be."

"That would be nice. Dad isn't supposed to be home until Monday at the earliest, so we could go out somewhere, just the two of us. Maybe that little Italian place we used to like." That little Italian place had been closed for almost two years. The last time we had gone was on my fifteenth birthday.

Dad had met us there after work. When dinner was over and the bill was paid, he told Mom he had a surprise for me. Why didn't Mom go on home? He wanted to take me to get my last present. We would see her later. I should have known better.

My gift was some ridiculous CD at a discount music store. He claimed it had meant a lot to him in his teenage years, and he thought I would appreciate it, too. His gift to himself was he got to fondle my knee the whole way to the store and on the way home. It was dark when we pulled into the driveway. He gave me a 'birthday kiss'. I hadn't spent a birthday with them since.

On my sixteenth birthday, I feigned illness. They had already told me they were getting me a car but hadn't found the right one yet. I begged for a MINI Cooper (I became obsessed with them after seeing The Italian Job a few years earlier). Mom said not a chance. They were impractical and way too expensive for a sixteen-year-old, even a used one. Dad said he tended to agree with her.

Because of the expense of a car and insurance, there weren't any gifts to unwrap, so I spent the evening in bed watching stupid movies on cable. That weekend I went out with Maggie, and we got blitzed. A week later my car showed up in the driveway—a three year old, cherry red MINI Cooper.

Mom was furious. She said it was too new for a sixteen-year-old, and I would wreck it in a week. She asked Dad through clenched teeth what happened to the ten year old Honda they looked at a few days before. Dad gave me a wink and a pat on the butt when he put the keys in my hand. I hated the car, too.

The next year I pretended to forget it was even my birthday. Mom couldn't understand how someone could forget her own birthday. I couldn't understand how she could be so naive.

For my eighteenth birthday, I was trying to figure out how to have a funeral instead of a party.

"Yeah, well maybe. I'm gonna shower and get going, Mom. Have a good day."

"Love you, sweetie."

"Uh huh."

It took Ken longer to answer the door than usual. I had to ring twice before I heard footsteps inside.

"Don't you have any patience, girl?"

"Sorry, sir." He looked disheveled. "I didn't wake you, did I?"

"No." Ken held the door open wider so I could slip in under his arm.

"Did you bring me anything?" He looked at the backpack slung over my shoulder. It reminded me of the scene in *The Wizard of Oz*—*I don't think there's anything in that black bag for me.* I couldn't help but chuckle at the comparison of petite, innocent Judy Garland to the giant in front of me.

"If you mean candy, it's in my bag. Don't tell me you've gone through all of those already?" I couldn't believe my nerve at even the smallest attempt to tease him. I half-expected to get backhanded right there and then. Part of me wanted him to.

"Nope. The peanut butter gnomes must have gotten them." Holy shit, was he actually being playful?

"Well, you better keep a closer eye on these."

"I'll try. Sneaky little buggers." I laughed, and I think he did, too. At least it was something like laughter. It sounded like a noise he was vaguely familiar with but wasn't accustomed to. So maybe he wasn't a maniac serial killer preying on unsuspecting girls. Maybe dying at the hands of another wasn't in the cards for me. But this was kind of nice, too.

We walked into the living room together and settled into our chairs. Before I could pick up the book, Ken said, "You're a senior this year." It wasn't a question.

"Yes, sir."

"What are you going to do after you graduate?" What was this sudden interest in my life? I was in no mood for a what-do-you-want-to-be-when-you-grow-up discussion. Maybe it was because I had no intention of making it that far. I had a life expectancy of twenty-one at most.

"Go to college, I guess."

"Where?"

"I don't know. I've been meaning to send in some applications. I haven't decided yet." Seriously, did we have to do this? It was bad enough that my counselor asked me on almost a daily basis where I was going. And heaven forbid my parents found out I had missed the deadlines for at least a dozen scholarships. The deadline for state financial aid had passed the week before and the federal deadline was only six weeks away. I guess it was another step in my quest for self-destruction.

"I see." Ken folded his hands in his lap and stared at me, waiting for something. I had nothing else to say on the subject, so I began reading. He was quick to fall asleep, and I was grateful. My head was full of warring emotions, and I could barely get through a sentence without screwing something up.

I was pissed that I'd been given the third degree. I was confused why he even cared and kind of touched he was curious about my future. Tsunami-sized waves of guilt were crashing over me because I knew I was systematically destroying said future. And then I got pissed all over again because I wasn't supposed to care either way. I wasn't going to have one anyway, right?

Dad's car was parked in the driveway when I got home, so I had two immediate reasons to feel furious. Because of the way he parked, my only option was the street. I hated parking in the street. I was utterly convinced it was only a matter of time before my MINI was sideswiped by some drunken country club socialite on her way home from playing Mahjong by the pool. I still loathed the car and everything it meant, but it didn't change the fact it was my only mode of transportation.

Second, he was home early. I was prepared for him to arrive on Monday night. It took effort to sink myself into the deep emotional void needed to deal with his presence. I didn't have the reserve strength built up. I was tempted to turn around and head straight over to Maggie's. She always welcomed me with open arms.

Then I saw Mom through the window. She was slumped on the couch, her head in her hands—everything about her cried defeat. She needed me. Well, she needed someone—someone to help her bear the load of having him in the house. I couldn't abandon her. I gathered my nerve and went in.

Mom looked up when I opened the door. Her eyes were red and puffy. Good Lord, he was home for a few hours and had already made her cry. Awesome.

"Hey, Mom."

"Hi, honey. Your dad's home." When she was okay with him, he was Dad. When they were fighting or he upset her, he was "your dad". As if he somehow belonged to me, and I was responsible.

"Yeah, I saw his car. What's he doing home so early?" My accusatory tone made it sound like it was her fault he was in our house. I guess it pretty much was. She married the son of a bitch.

"Apparently they didn't need him after all. There's a new guy they're giving some accounts to, and this was one of them."

It was inappropriate to take such pleasure in the knowledge Dad was getting screwed at work. Oh well, no one ever accused me of being appropriate.

"Didn't he know that before he flew all the way down there?"

"Of course I did. I'm not stupid!" Dad's voice shot down the hallway and straight into my gut. He followed right behind it. "But that little shit has no idea how to handle an account this size. There was no way in hell I was going to let some wet behind the ears, fresh out of college punk fuck up one of the biggest accounts we have."

I didn't point out the obvious—if the kid was so green, Dad would still be down there holding his hand. He wouldn't have been sent home.

"Maybe if your mother could take better care of things around here, I wouldn't be so distracted while I'm on the road. I wouldn't be losing accounts to some asshole kid." He was distracted on the road, alright, but it wasn't by thoughts of home. It was the little HR gal with her hand in his lap. Once again, I refrained from pointing out the obvious.

"Darren, I am doing the best I can, and I don't see how a few dirty dishes should have any bearing on -"

"You don't understand much of anything, do you? I bust my ass, on the road day after day, so you can go shopping, and out to eat, and buy her—" he pointed at me "—anything she goddamn wants. Jesus, I even pay for someone to come clean this house twice a month. How challenging is it to keep it clean the rest of the time?"

Dad swallowed his bottom lip—a sure sign an epic shit storm was about to hit our house. My stomach flipped, and I knew where this was going—screaming and crying, accusations and slammed doors. Sometimes he would back my mom against a wall and punch holes next to her head. He had done it to me once or twice. It would have been better if he had just hit me instead of leaving me there waiting— waiting to see if he would come back, wondering if the next time he would actually let his fist fly into my face. I wasn't going to stick around and watch it. Not this time.

I went down the stairs and straight out the back door. As I walked around the neighborhood, the sun started to set, illuminating the sky in deep reds and purples. I tried to stop and appreciate the beauty of it. All I could think was, *It's a damn sunset. Happens every night. Who gives a shit?*

Dusk turned to full darkness while I walked and smoked. Eventually my feet landed me in front of Ken's house. It was wrong— I knew it before I even stepped into the front yard, but I couldn't help it.

There was a single light coming from the small bay window. Through the mini-blinds I could see him sitting in an old wing back chair. I crept closer to the window, curious for a glimpse of his life beyond John Irving and candy.

The walls were covered in old photos and memorabilia of his time in the Marines. I saw a full dress uniform hanging on a coat rack, a shadow box with medals, and a huge woven tapestry with the Marine emblem in the middle on the wall behind him. In his hands was another photo. I knew by the silver frame it was the one from the living room—the one of him and the girl.

In the harsh light of the floor lamp, I could see tears running down his cheeks. It was the silent, unashamed crying of someone who thinks they are alone. It was heart-breaking.

I'm not sure how long I stood there watching his private grief. It was a horrible invasion of his privacy and borderline illegal, but I couldn't turn away. That was until I heard a gruff voice and the deep-throated rumble of a very large dog behind me.

"What do you think you're doing?" I was so startled I fell against the window, causing Ken's head to jerk up. *Well shit.*

"Nothing. I mean, I just… I know Ken and I…" There wasn't a single answer that was going to make this look any better. The front porch light came on. *Shit again.*

"Who's out there?"

"It's Bill, Ken, from down the street. I caught some punk looking in your window."

Punk? Really? I was in sweatpants and a t-shirt—Abercrombie & Fitch at that. There was nothing about me that said punk. Well, except I was lurking outside some old guy's window. That leaned toward punkish, I suppose.

"She says she knows you. Might want to call the cops." Well, that seemed over the top. My only choice was to step into the little island of light on the front walk and face the music.

"Hi, Ken. It's me, Persephone." Ken looked at me, confused. Great, he didn't have a freaking clue who I was. Shit, was he really going to call the cops?

"Oh yeah, Persephone. Uh, come on in. We're fine, Bill."

"Well, if you're sure." Bill looked far from convinced.

"Go home, Bill." Ha ha, Bill got *his* nose thumped. I tried to hide my smirk—served the asshole right for trying to get me into trouble. I ducked under Ken's arm and into the house. He closed the door, turned, and stared at me.

"I'm really sorry. I was out walking, and I saw your light on, and I wasn't trying to sneak or anything."

"What are you doing out this late? Where are your parents?" Of course that would be his first question. Ken wasn't raised in a world where parents let their kids wander alone after dark. Especially their daughters.

"My parents are fighting. I didn't want to listen to it anymore." The truth was out of my mouth before I could think of a lie. It sounded so boring and trite, even to my ears. I couldn't imagine how it would sound to a man who had fought in at least one major war. He probably thought I was some spoiled brat whose mommy and daddy were squabbling over which size jetted tub to put in the master suite. That would have been a great lie.

Ken kept staring at me, causing me to babble more truths. "I'm not really sure why I ended up here. Like I said I was just walking. I hate being home when he's there. I had to get out."

He nodded a single time, as if coming to a decision. "Alright then. The blanket's next to the chair. I don't have any extra pillows, but the recliner is pretty soft. Leave the bathroom light on. I don't like walking out into the dark. Goodnight, Persephone." So I was supposed to stay? It was certainly better than the alternative—a night of sleeping with one eye open, my body on high alert waiting for my late night visitor.

It was only a little after nine. Would my parents check on me? What would they do if they found I wasn't there? I knew the answer to that question before it even formed. Mom would never make it out of her room. Dad would make sure she was too wrapped up in her own misery to worry about me. As for Dad... there was a good chance he would wander down at some point, but he would probably think I was at Maggie's. I heard Ken's bedroom door close.

There was no way I would be able to go to sleep so early. It would be hours before I would even be close to tired. But what else was I going to do? Shrugging, I went into the living room and snuggled into the recliner. Ken was right—I didn't need a pillow. The blanket smelled like vanilla and sandalwood—the way a girl should remember her father. Instead I would remember sweat and foul, panting breath.

I fell into a deep, dreamless sleep almost immediately. When the sun broke through the back window the next morning, I got up as quietly as I could, assuming Ken would still be in bed. The house was silent.

On the front table was another envelope with my name on it.

Let yourself out and lock the door behind you. This is your key so you won't have to trespass anymore. I will see you this afternoon.

Trespassing! I wasn't trespassing! I was just… Okay, maybe I was. But how presumptuous to think I would be back in the afternoon. What if I had plans? I mean, I didn't, and I would come back, but still.

When I got home, my house was as silent as Ken's. Sunday mornings were sleep-in mornings. I wouldn't see my parents until well after noon, if at all. Dad would stay holed up in his room until hunger drove him into the kitchen. Mom would probably stay in bed until the cleaning lady showed up on Monday.

As a little girl, I would take her a cup of coffee first thing on Sunday mornings. I would curl up beside her in bed, and Mom would trade me the remote for the mug. We would snuggle and watch cartoons, just Mom and me, even on the weekends Dad was home. During those quiet hours, I could pretend there wasn't a world outside the sanctuary of her room.

In the shower I thought about the night before. I felt so rested. I couldn't remember the last time I had slept through the night—no nightmares, no late night visitors, nothing. I didn't realize how worn down I was until I got a taste of real sleep. It wasn't only the sleep. There was something else, even if I couldn't figure out what it was. I wanted more.

8.

"Hi, James, it's me, Persephone." It was early afternoon, and I was driving around before going back over to Ken's house. As I suspected, there had been no sighting of my parents. I had, however, failed to text Maggie back when she asked if I wanted to grab coffee at Classic Rock. Oh well, she would understand.

"Well, hey there, Miss Persephone. How are things in your neck of the woods?"

"I'm doing okay." I didn't know if I should tell James about the night before. On one hand, was it any of his business his friend let an unhappy teenage girl stay in his house? James would want to know why, what happened to lead me there. He would have questions I didn't want to answer, and I wasn't sure I would be able to lie. God knows I was no longer capable of lying to Ken. What if James was the same way?

On the other hand, if I didn't tell him and Ken did, would James think it was weird that I didn't say anything? Would he assume I was trying to hide something? I was, of course, but I didn't need him to know that.

"So you had kinda a rough night, huh, sweet pea?" Well that solved that problem. Apparently Ken had already spoken to him.

"Yeah, it was a weird deal. I hope I didn't make Ken uncomfortable. It just kinda happened, you know?"

"Oh sure. I'm glad you two are taking care of each other. Is he doin' okay?" *Taking care of each other.* It had a nice ring to it.

"Yeah, I think so. We're getting along alright."

"Well, good. You know, Persephone, I…" There was a long pause I wasn't sure if I should interrupt or not. "The thing with Ken is—you know what? Never mind." *The thing with Ken is he killed people for the CIA? He was a drug dealer and is now in witness protection? He has split personalities—watch out for the cross-dressing Latin princess one? What?* The suspense was killing me.

"What is it?"

"Seriously, it's no big deal. So when are you going back over there?"

I wanted to scream. Why are adults such a pain in the ass? Even the good ones? Jesus. "I'm actually on my way there now. Almost in the driveway."

"That's great. How 'bout you give me a holler sometime next week? Let me know how things are going?"

"Fine, will do." I sounded bitchy, but I couldn't help it. What a shitty thing to do to someone. I wouldn't be able to think about anything else the rest of the day. Dammit, why wouldn't he finish his sentence?

"You take care, Persephone. Talk to you soon."

"Yep." I hung up before James had a chance to respond. *So there.*

Ken was sitting in the same room as the night before, staring at the wall. I cleared my throat, trying not to scare him.

"Hello, sir."

"Hello, Persephone. I was just walking through the past. Are you ready?" His old knees cracked as he rose from his chair, and he winced.

"Um, yeah, sure. Are you okay?"

"I'm fine. I'm always fine." His tone sounded way too much like mine when I wanted to be left the hell alone.

We spent the next two hours trying to lose ourselves in the world of the boy with the wrecked voice and his best friend Johnny. It didn't work for either of us. When my throat was dry and mouth too tired to keep going, I finally looked up from the page. Ken was still wide awake.

Now what? He was always asleep when I left. I had no idea how to wrap this up with him staring at me like that.

"I think that's enough for today, Persephone."

"Oh, okay. When would you like me to come back?"

"Whenever you want to. I'm not going anywhere."

"I guess I could come tomorrow after school."

He raised his eyebrows. "That soon? Don't you have any friends? Something to do besides come over here?" His bluntness took me by surprise. I should have been offended, but Ken sounded legitimately concerned there was nothing else in my life. It was the tone that kept me from snapping back at him with a pithy comment about having much better things to do.

The sad truth was, other than Maggie, I didn't have anyone else. And there was nothing else for me to do. I was actually beginning to like Ken. Not everyone in the world would let some strange teenager crash at their house for the night, no questions asked.

"No, I guess I don't."

"Monday will be fine then. Goodbye, Persephone."

"Bye, Ken."

I didn't want to go home, but I didn't want to be out in public. The unusual ending to the afternoon, the thing unsaid by James, my own thoughts—everything felt so wrong. Outside, my car felt too open. I was exposed and there was too much air to breathe. My car was too small and cramped—it felt like the seatbelt was cutting off my circulation. I couldn't handle going home. There was a good chance both my parents would be up and around, and I didn't want to face them. I pulled up Maggie's number on my phone but didn't know what to say to her.

I drove around as long as I could. My brain could not wrap itself around the fact Ken actually seemed to care about me. It didn't make sense. I finally realized it didn't matter why he cared, only that he did. That was enough. I flipped the last cigarette from my pack out the window and pointed my car towards home.

"Persephone, I thought we had a discussion about you coming and going as you please. Didn't we?" I couldn't figure out if he was talking about the fact I wasn't there the night before or if it was because I was walking in at nine at night. Either way, I didn't care.

I shrugged. "Yeah, I guess we did. Sorry about that."

"Sorry about that? Do you think that's an acceptable response to the fact I came down to check on my daughter last night, and she was not in her bed? Do you know what that was like? To not have any idea where you were?"

Yes, it must have been excruciating, I'm sure. All revved up and ready to play only to find your favorite toy missing. Absolutely tragic.

I couldn't explain what came over me at that moment. Natural instinct was to duck and cover, mumble through an apology and get as far away as fast as possible. But from somewhere inside, a person I didn't know existed reared up and said, "Check on me? Really? Since when do you come down to *check on me*? Does Mom know you were *checking on me*?"

I had never seen fear on his face before, and I don't think it was exactly fear I saw this time. Shock, maybe? He looked like a child who had fallen, scraped his knee and was trying to decide if tears were the most proper, profitable response.

"Listen, Persephone—"

"Leave me alone." With that, I hitched my backpack over my shoulder and walked down the stairs as my dad stood there, opening and closing his mouth like a guppy. Damn if it didn't feel good.

9.

Two nights later, I showed up at Ken's front door again. At first, I wasn't sure what brought me there. Dad was on a trip. Mom was passed out. There was no drama, nothing to run away from. When I put my key in the door, I realized what it was. Safety. Comfort. I had to know those feelings were still there—that they weren't something I had imagined. I wanted something I could hold on to.

Ken was sitting in his recliner as if he were waiting for me. When I walked in, he got up, nodded once, patted my head, and went to his own room. He didn't ask for an explanation, and I didn't offer one. He accepted me as a part of his home, his routine. That night I slept holding on to the key he had given me. There was an impression of it in my palm the next morning that didn't fade completely until almost lunch.

Over the next few weeks, I spent the night several more times and was there every other afternoon to read. James and I talked often, but he never broached the subject of Ken's big secret again. I didn't ask.

Whatever it was, I didn't want to know. I wanted everything to stay the same—safe and unshaken.

Most mornings when I woke at Ken's house, I would find a fresh cup of coffee waiting for me on the entry table. One morning, two weeks before the deadline, I found an application for federal student aid, obviously downloaded off a website. *So you have a computer hidden around here, you little sneak.* I was too amused to be angry. I filled it out the same night and stuck it in the mail. Ken never asked about it, but he did look a little Cheshire cat-ish over the next few days.

We fell into a nice routine. It was comforting and stable. I knew Ken would always be there when I walked in the front door. James always answered when I called. Happy wasn't exactly a word I was familiar with, but I thought this must have been pretty damn close.

One particular morning, I was almost on the verge of admitting life might actually have some value—my life specifically. The sun was warming everything it touched, almost as if it was smiling down on the world. I had a cigarette hanging out the window and not a single fresh cut on my body. It was as close to perfect a day as possible. Stupid me actually thought it would last.

There were pop quizzes in two of my classes I was woefully unprepared for, Maggie seemed cranky and off-kilter every time I tried to talk to her, and the strap on my backpack broke during lunch. In the grand scheme of things, they were minor irritations. But they were enough to bring me to breaking point even before Mom called.

"Hey, Mom, what's up?"

"I need you to come straight home after school. No sneaking off to wherever you have been hiding out the past few weeks. Straight home, young lady." *What the hell?*

"Uh, sure. What's going on? Is everything okay?"

"We need to talk about a few things." Well shit, now what had I done?

"Ten four. On my way then." No goodbye, drive carefully or I love you. Just the click of the phone. She obviously had her temper up about something. God only knew what.

When I walked in the door, she was perched on the edge of the couch, hands clenching and unclenching.

"So what exactly have you been doing?"

"I'm sorry?"

"Oh, I'm sure you *should* be sorry. Now you tell me what you're sorry for."

"I don't have a clue. Really, Mom. I don't know what you're talking about."

"I am well aware of the fact you have been sneaking off somewhere after school. I also know you have been out overnight—without permission, I might add—at least twice in the past week. So once again, what exactly have you been doing?"

Holy hell, he had done it again. My father's favorite trick was to bitch and complain to Mom about something until she finally had enough and came after me. It kept us in an almost constant state of conflict, focused on each other instead of him. I should have known I hadn't shut him down—he'd sent in the reserve troops.

"Mom, I haven't been doing anything. I may not have been in bed when Dad came down, but I was just out walking. I wasn't gone overnight."

"At three in the morning? Do you think I'm stupid?" Obviously Dad didn't give her much credit for intelligence if he actually admitted to being in my room at three in the morning. Why didn't she question him on what he was doing there in the first place?

"Mom, calm down. I really haven't been doing anything wrong. I promise. I don't know what Dad has told you—"

"Your father has nothing to do with this." *Yeah right.* "I am capable of being a parent without his help." *Actually you're a better parent when he isn't helping. You're a better you, for that matter.* But that was something I could only think and not say, unfortunately.

"I know, Mom. That's not what I meant. I'm just saying if Dad thinks I've been out overnight he's wrong. As for where I go after school, I'm out with friends, like I always am."

"Persephone Ann Daniels, I am going to give you one last chance to come clean with me. I think you have some boy you're hiding and lying about, and I will not have it." How funny she was so close to the truth, except "the boy" was a seventy year old man.

"Mom, there is no boy. I haven't been on a date in at least six months, and you know it." It was true. Between combating home life, trying to maintain my grades to ensure graduation, and now Ken, a boyfriend was a distraction I didn't need at that moment. Plus I never kept a boy around for long—maybe three months if he was really lucky.

I learned the hard way my sophomore year that after three months, relationships got too intense for my liking. Don't get me wrong, the kissing was nice, as long as he realized he didn't need to imitate a puppy and slobber all over my face. But around the ninety day mark, feeling me up under my shirt wasn't good enough. He wanted full access, and why did I keep pushing his hand away every time it trailed below my waistline? God, the way a high school boy whined could put a two-year-old to shame.

The boy I dated my sophomore year actually remained patient until well into the fifth month. I knew it wasn't love, but it was the closest thing two fifteen-year-olds could feel to love. He made me feel special. He was gentle. He seemed to intuitively know where my boundaries were and didn't try to cross them. Until that damn fifth month.

He started with gentle prodding that became more insistent with each date. I finally gave in. Part of me wanted to shut him up, part of me thought it was my obligation (he had, after all, put up with so much from me and been so sweet up until then), and, let's be honest, I was fifteen. Part of me really wanted to. I wanted to know what it was like to be touched with gentleness and affection.

So the shirt came off, followed quickly by the bra. It was humiliating. He immediately started touching the scars and quizzing me about the fresh cut on my shoulder. He wanted to know what happened, why were there marks all over my torso? I didn't have any good answers. I told him it was none of his business. That wasn't good enough. I told him to take me home. That was fine with him.

We saw each other in the hallway the following Monday. He was holding hands with some cheerleader. I took it as his way of breaking up with me. To his credit, I don't think he ever told anyone the real reason we stopped dating. Thank God. But I learned my lesson. Three months was the limit.

"Go to your room, Persephone. You're grounded until you can decide to be honest with me. I can't believe you think this is acceptable." I wanted to argue. I wanted to cry and scream and tell her where I was at night and why. I wanted to tell her that her husband was the reason I was running off—the only guy her daughter was lying about was her own father. But what good would it do? I would be gone soon. With any luck, I would be a few blocks away in the National

Place Cemetery or thousands of miles away at college. Just a few more months one way or the other, and I would escape.

Anyway, it wasn't like Mom would remember for more than an hour she had grounded me. Dad was due home from his trip, and she would have other things to focus on. Apparently, so would I. There would be no escaping to Ken's. *Dear God, just make it quick. Please.*

I didn't bother closing my door—not even when I was tracing little cuts across my stomach, reopening old scars, making new ones. I heard the front door open on hash mark number five and my parents talking in Mom's room during cuts seven through eleven. I stopped at fifteen and laid a towel over my stomach. It would soak up the blood until it clotted.

At midnight, he was in my doorway. "So you're still here. Mom told me she grounded you." I stared at him. "That's a shame." He sat down on the edge of my bed, cupping my face in his hand.

"I told her she was being too hard on you. Teenagers will be teenagers. You need a little bit of freedom. She just wouldn't listen. I tried to get you out of it, honey." When I was younger, I fell for this good cop/bad cop thing. I really thought my mother was the shrew and Dad was trying to be a good parent. If I would just let him touch me here, kiss me there then he made sure I got what I wanted. He made Mom be nicer to me, stop yelling at me all the time. Sure enough, the day after a late night visit to my room, the punishment was lifted or the new shirt I wanted would appear. Funny thing, I never enjoyed it much once I got it.

There was one time when I was ten. Everyone I knew was getting a new gaming system for Christmas. I wanted one so badly. I begged and whined every chance I got. Mom flat out put her foot down. There was no way I was turning into some zombie sitting in front of the TV all day. She said if I asked one more time I was grounded. I was ten. Of course I asked one more time. Multiple more times, in fact. I got yelled at. I got grounded. I got told I probably wouldn't get any Christmas presents at all. This was two weeks before Christmas and the night before Dad got home from a trip.

When he came home his first order of business, after getting the rundown from Mom, was to come to my room. I was savvy enough to know how this went. He got what he wanted, and I would get what I wanted. I didn't even have to wait until Christmas. The system was waiting for me the next day when I got off the bus. I played with it three times and then told Mom to sell it. She never said a word.

It wasn't until I got older I realized these situations were his creations—playing Mom and me off each other like chess pieces. Knowing it didn't help. I was too numb to do anything about it.

"I know I've been gone a lot lately. It's rough on Mom when she has to take care of you by herself. She doesn't love you like I do. You're so special to me." He leaned down to kiss my nose. "You know that, right? You know how much I love you?"

The silence was filled with touching and kissing and tears. I tried not to react. I tried to stay still and silent, but when his fingers brushed against the fresh cuts on my stomach I cried out. "Shhh, your mom is sleeping. You know how cranky she gets when you wake her up." He didn't even notice the smear of blood on his hand.

10.

I had to wear a dress to school the next day. There was no way a waistband was going over those cuts. Mom told me I looked nice as I was walking out the door. I silently told her to go to hell—at least I would have company.

About three blocks from the house I knew there was no way I was going to make it through the day around all those people and inane teachers. It felt like there was a slick layer of scum all over my body, and my head hurt. I had all of the symptoms of a hangover without any of the fun of drinking the night before.

I couldn't go back home. If Mom bought that I was sick, she might spend the whole day hovering over me. If she didn't believe me, I would only increase the odds my grounding would stick for more than twenty-four hours. Neither option appealed to me.

Maggie would already be settled into first hour, cell phone safely tucked away and silent in her purse. No way to get her to skip with me. Frankly, I didn't feel like being around her anyway. Or anyone else for that matter. Turning my car around, I hoped Ken wouldn't completely flip when I appeared at his front door.

I was tempted to use my key but didn't want to scare him showing up in the morning, unexpected. I knocked several times, shifting my weight from one foot to the other. After several minutes, he answered, looking out of sorts again. He was still in his robe and unshaven. I had never seen him like this and was suddenly, painfully reminded why my presence had first been requested by James in the first place. Ken was sick. Ken was dying. Like the first time we met, I fought the urge to run.

"Persephone! What are you doing here?" His face went from confusion to concern to I think embarrassment I caught him looking like hell.

"I'm sorry, Ken. I shouldn't have come. I couldn't handle school today, and I couldn't stay at home. I don't know. I'm sorry. I'll go." *And you're sick, and I don't know if I want to face that today, too. I'm scared. I need to be safe.*

"No, no. Come in. Go into the living room. I'll be there in a minute."

He shuffled down the hallway, and I heard the shower start. I wandered around the living room, looking at the photos again, skimming the books crammed into the shelves. One thing I had to give him, he certainly had an eclectic taste in reading material. There was everything from true crime, political biographies and philosophy to Stephen King and Amy Tan.

It wasn't long before Ken was back, clean shaven and presentable. "Have a seat, Persephone."

I could see it all over his face. We were about to have "the talk". I hated "the talk". I had been hearing versions of it since I was eleven. It would start with something about me being a bright girl with a good future if I would just "apply myself" and "stop being so unhappy all the time." I had a good life with "no reason to be so angry *all the time.*"

Dammit, it was so unfair. Why couldn't a single person in my life see what was really going on? Why didn't they care? I perched on the edge of my rocking chair, ready to bolt the minute he started in. Sick or not, I was so tempted to tell him to save it before he even got started. The rage was building rapidly from my stomach, rising into my chest and throat. I was either going to scream or throw up.

"The book is next to your chair. You don't have your Diet Coke. Do you need something to drink before we start?" What the hell? Did he have no idea I was supposed to be in school? Was he completely confused?

"Um, no. I'm fine."

"Okay. I think we should be able to finish before lunch. There isn't much left." He settled back in his chair. So I read. It was close to noon when I read, "O God—please give him back! I shall keep asking You."

I looked up to find Ken wide awake, wiping the back of his hand across his cheek. It made me feel less self-conscious about having to do the same.

"Are you hungry?" Ken asked. I nodded. "Great. Let's go make some sandwiches. Is turkey okay?" I nodded again, still braced for the lecture that apparently wasn't coming. "Well, come on then. They're not going to make themselves."

I was used to the turkey sandwiches at my house—if you could call them that. They were usually constructed with dry turkey on close to stale bread. If I was really lucky I could scrounge some not-quite expired mayo from the back of the fridge. Grocery shopping wasn't high on Mom's priority list, unless the liquor cabinet was looking low.

I sometimes wondered what it was like to have meals prepared by someone who loved you rather than the staff at the nearest take-out place.

Ken's turkey sandwiches, on the other hand, were a work of art. It was a huge stack of bread, turkey, avocado, tomato, mayo and cheese. There was no way I was going to eat all of it.

"Milk or water?" Before I could answer, Ken said, "Milk. I bet you don't get enough calcium. Grab a bag of chips out of the pantry."

We ate for several minutes in complete silence. Finally I said, "Ken, I'm supposed to be in school right now." For the love of God, why couldn't I keep my mouth shut around him?

"I know." He picked around the edges of his sandwich, eating ingredients instead of taking real bites.

"It's not like there is much going on right now. I mean, there's only a couple of weeks left. Not even that really. My teachers probably haven't even noticed I'm not there."

"Okay."

"I just didn't want you to think I was going to get in trouble or miss any work. It's pretty much over. I've already gotten accepted to a couple of schools. Finals are next week, but I only have to take two." In most of the honors classes, if you carried a solid A and had 95% attendance, you weren't required to take the final. I only had to take one in Calculus and my stupid health class. I had put that particular requirement off until the last possible semester. It was a horrid class filled with freshmen, but at least the final would be easy.

"Really? I wasn't aware you had gotten acceptance letters yet. Have you decided where you are going?" It was if he was asking about the weather—completely casual and non-committal. Was he luring me into a false sense of security before he pounced? When was he going to lay into me about my irresponsibility?

"Well, I got into UMKC and MU in Columbia, but I don't think I want to go to either one of those. Even though they gave me pretty decent scholarships. I also got into OU, in Oklahoma? The scholarships aren't as good, but they count Missouri residents as in-state tuition. I'll have to use the loans I got approved for, which I don't really want to, but you know… And I'll probably have to get a job while I'm there. But it'll be okay. It's farther away from home, and the campus looks great. I guess they have a pretty good football team, so that's fun. And…" I realized I was babbling at this point, and Ken was staring at me, his lunch forgotten on his plate. "Uh, yeah, so anyway."

"Do your parents know you are going to school out-of-state?" I wasn't sure my parents were even aware I was graduating soon. I mean, Mom had ridden me pretty hard at the start of the year about getting my shit together, picking a school and all that stuff, but like most things, it was a short-lived obsession. It required way too much energy on her part. She hadn't mentioned it in several weeks. And Dad, well, Dad only cared about one thing when it came to me, and where I was going to college wasn't it. The only thing that mattered to me was that I was far out of his reach when fall rolled around.

"No, not yet. But they're not gonna care. They just want to make sure I get a good education." There, that was a good response. That's what a normal kid would say, right? As if Ken had any misconceptions about my screwed up little family. Right, because a normal kid would often run off to a near stranger's house on a regular basis.

"Uh huh. So they won't be helping with the cost?"

"Probably not. I like to do things for myself." I shuddered to think what tuition from my parents would *actually* cost me.

"I see. What are you going to do this summer once school is out? You only have two weeks left, correct?"

"Not sure yet. I might need to get a job, get some money saved up."

"Hmm. Alright then. Could I trouble you to clean up the lunch mess, Persephone? I'm a little tired. You can stay here the rest of the afternoon if you would like. Help yourself to anything to eat or drink." He had only eaten a third of his sandwich.

"Yeah, sure, not a problem." I heard Ken's bedroom door shut and pushed myself back from the table. As I rinsed dishes and put away all the sandwich stuff, I tried to figure out what Ken's angle was. Why hadn't he gotten on to me? Why wasn't he asking me more questions? Wasn't he curious why I was at his house so much? I switched back and forth from being relieved he minded his own business to being hurt he didn't care enough to ask.

After clean-up, I was at a loss what to do next. I couldn't go home. I didn't want to leave. I didn't feel like reading, although my options were almost limitless with Ken's bookshelves. I wandered through the living room, picking up photos but not really looking at them, running my fingers over the spines of books and finally, with nothing else to do, I stood in the middle of the living room, staring at the wall.

As I often did when I found myself restless or bored, my fingers began trailing along the scars on my arms. I began with the ones at my wrist, pushing my watch out of the way to feel them. Next the crooks of my elbows. Finally, I found the thick one along my right shoulder.

I remembered that one. I remembered it well. It had been deeper than most. It wouldn't stop bleeding, and I was terrified it would need stitches. I had gone through almost an entire box of gauze pads trying to make it stop.

All I had really wanted to do was lie down and close my eyes. The lack of sleep combined with the loss of blood had exhausted me. But I also knew I couldn't leave those bloody bandages and rags in my room. Nor could I throw them away at the house. The fallout of this cut was enough to actually raise suspicion. I dragged myself out to my car, drove to the gas station, and threw them in the dumpster.

On the way home my eyes refused to stay open, and I swerved into the other lane, almost colliding with a large work truck. The driver laid on his horn, jerking me awake in time to get out of his way. Only after I got home did I realize what a golden opportunity I had missed. My MINI would have been no match for his several tons of steel. Natural instinct to avoid danger had gotten in the way again.

After the scar on my shoulder, I felt for the one on my left hip. It was so thick I could feel it through my dress. It wrapped all the way around from my butt to inner thigh. If it wasn't so morbid, I would have almost been impressed by that one. It took real dedication to cut like that.

There had been no mapping, no rituals, no anything that night. In a moment of desperation, pain beyond any human threshold rolling through my body, I had snatched a razor and simply sliced. There was so much disgust and shame welling up inside I didn't think I would ever be able to bleed it all out. I didn't even register the pain for a good sixty seconds.

When my leg started throbbing, and I saw how much blood was pouring out I knew I should be panicked. This could finally be it. For all the attacks on my wrists, it could be this cut—not even across a major artery—that would end it. How ironic. The temporary fix could have become the permanent cure.

In the end, my body betrayed me. I did nothing to stop the blood. I lay down on my bed and let it bleed. It clotted on its own, after soaking my sheets. I threw them away on the way to school the next morning. There was nothing I could do about the stain on my mattress. Good thing about being a girl—built-in excuse for bloodstains.

And then there were the fresh cuts across my stomach. When I touched them through my dress, the fabric scratched painfully against them. They were shallow enough I wasn't really worried about them opening back up, but deep enough they would probably always be with me.

Some of the scars had faded over the years. Some seemed like they would never heal. Some I could tie to a specific event or time. Some were there to remind me of who and what I was. There were days I didn't know if I could define myself without those marks on my body. They were mine and only mine. If I didn't add to the collection, would I stop being me? Was there a chance I could be someone else? Someone better?

Suddenly, I was exhausted. I didn't want to think or feel anymore. I wanted to sleep. I curled up in what I now considered my recliner (even though Ken still sat there when we read) and pulled the old fleece blanket over me, all the way up to my nose. I went to sleep thinking of vanilla and sandalwood, cold steel and hurt.

11.

"Persephone. Wake up, Persephone." When I felt a hand on my shoulder gently shaking me awake my first instinct was to curl into a ball. Or punch. I squeezed my eyes shut, hoping if I pretended to be asleep he would go away. It very rarely worked.

"Persephone, it's time to get up." Then I remembered I wasn't at home, and it wasn't my father trying to rouse me. It was safe to wake up. I rolled my head around to look at Ken standing over me. I had no idea what time it was. Should I be at home? Was I late? I was supposedly grounded.

"Oh shit! What time is it?" I struggled to get out of the chair.

"Calm down. It's barely after two."

"Oh good. Um, I kind of got grounded yesterday. I'm supposed to go straight home after school."

"Grounded? For what?" *Because of you. Because my mom lets my dad play her like a chess game. Because I refuse to tell the truth to anyone but you. Because my family is completely screwed up.* Any of those answers would be truthful but none really acceptable.

"Mom thinks I've been sneaking around. She told me I couldn't do anything after school or on the weekends for a few weeks. Don't worry. She'll forget about it in a couple of days."

Ken sighed and sat in the rocking chair. "Perhaps it's time we talked. I think there are some things we both need to know about each other."

If he had caught me at any other time, if I hadn't just woken up, if I hadn't been emotionally exhausted from the night before, maybe I could have come up with something better. Maybe I could have kept the wall up with a perfect lie. Or maybe not.

"Mom drinks a lot. She is usually in bed by nine. And Dad travels for his job. Nobody keeps track of me all that much."

Ken took a moment to absorb what I'd said while he got up and walked over to the bookcase. He kept his back to me when he said, "I had a sister. She was four years younger than me."

Ken turned around, holding the photo of him and the girl. He handed it to me. "This is her when she was fourteen. I was getting ready to leave for boot camp. Her name was Rachel."

"She was beautiful."

"Yes, she was. This was the last time I saw her. While I was in Vietnam, Rachel was killed in a car accident."

"Oh, Ken, I'm so sorry."

He held up his hand. "Let me get through this. Before I shipped out, there was this guy coming around. Nick. A couple of years younger than me, couple of years older than Rachel. Our parents were hard workers, and my dad was a hard drinker. My mother did what she could, but she wasn't a very strong woman. I did my best to take care of Rachel, but I needed to get out. My father wasn't a good man, and he and I were coming to a head. One of us was going to get hurt and bad. He didn't much bother with Rachel, but there was something about me that got under his skin. When I was old enough, I signed up for the Marines.

"So back to Nick. He was a hood. If he hadn't flunked out of school by then, he was well on his way. The first time he showed up to the house smelling like whiskey I let him know he wasn't welcome around my sister. The second time I laid him out. I thought that was the end of it. After I left, I suppose he thought the way was clear. Rachel was lonely and sad. She started going around with him. He ran a stop sign one night and killed them both. I was somewhere I couldn't be reached. I didn't find out about it until months later. I missed her funeral."

"Ken, I didn't know. I mean, I thought when I saw the picture... That first night when I came over, I thought maybe she was..."

"The reason I told you all this, Persephone, is to let you know, I owe something to Rachel. I abandoned her when she needed me because I was selfish and wanted to get away. I will not do that again. So I have given this situation a lot of thought, and I think we need to come to a new arrangement."

My heart and stomach crawled into my throat, fighting for space. I couldn't breathe. New arrangement? What did that mean? An "arrangement" like I had with my father? I knew it! Goddammit, I knew it was coming! How did I let myself actually believe that this time was different? They always wanted something in return. There was always a catch. *Fuck it. Bring it on. You can have whatever you want, and I can have what I want. The strength to finally finish the job. I hate you.*

"Um, okay." I tried to keep my voice calm and even.

"I think you should move in here." I stared at him. He couldn't have possibly said what I thought he did. What price tag was attached? What did he *really* want? I waited. "This is what I've come up with. I would like to hire you between now and when you leave for college. I would like you to be my in-home caregiver. Let me tell you what I expect, and then you can let me know what you think."

And here it was—what he *expected*. "Uh…okay. I mean, I don't know what to say."

"I will expect you here every night by five. You will have from two in the afternoon on Saturdays until two on Sundays off. I will need you to do some cooking, some cleaning, reading obviously, grocery shopping, that kind of thing. I will provide room and board and pay you two hundred and fifty dollars a week. You have about fourteen weeks left before you leave for school. That will give you around $3,500. That should cover your books and some of your living expenses for the first year. Would you like the job?"

There was no manipulation or intimidation. Ken was looking me in the eye, his face serious and sincere. Was this my chance? Was there really another way out? I swallowed my natural instinct to respond 'Hell yeah!' and instead said, "Yes, sir."

"Do you think your parents would allow it?" There wasn't a chance in hell.

"I don't know."

"I would like you to start moving your stuff in this weekend. There is a spare bedroom you can have. It has a bed, dresser, and," his voice caught before he continued, "some other stuff we can move out. You'll probably want new sheets and that kind of thing. You can decorate it however you would like."

And then it hit me. What about my piano? I couldn't possibly leave my music behind. And it would be impossible to move it over here. My parents would never agree to pay a professional moving company. Even if I did figure out a way to bring it, when would I play it? What if Ken hated music? His life was quiet.

Did he realize it wouldn't be quiet anymore? I would have to shower at his house. Eat there. Do homework. My clothes would have to be washed. My phone would be ringing and pinging with texts. What if I had a nightmare? I hadn't yet in all the nights I had stayed there, but what if I did?

Then the ultimate question sliced through my brain—what about my most important habit? My first and strongest love. Would the razors come with me, too? Would I still need them? Could I hide it from Ken?

"Come on, I'll show you your room." With all of this still bubbling in my head like a poisonous brew in a cauldron, I followed Ken down the small hallway, past the corner bedroom I found him in what seemed like a lifetime ago, to a door I assumed led to my new bedroom.

Ken opened it and waved for me to go in. I stopped at the threshold, breath, heartbeat, brain function, everything slamming to a halt. Against the wall was an old Baldwin upright with a matching bench.

"It was my sister's. She played beautifully." I barely heard him as I crossed the room and lifted the lid. There wasn't a single speck of dust on it. From the outside it seemed incredibly well-cared for. I pressed a key. The note was true. The sheet music for 'Amazing Grace' was lying open.

Without asking I sat down and began to play. The melody filled the room, sweet and clear. I didn't realize I was crying until the final note faded.

Ken placed his hand on my shoulder. "Welcome home, Persephone."

12.

Mom and Dad were both home when I got there. Dad must have taken off early. He was tapping away on his phone, most likely sexting the little chippie from his office, and Mom was staring at a glass that was little more than melting ice. I could only hope this was at least the second drink of the day. They both looked up when I walked in.

"Hey, guys."

"Hi, honey. How was school?" Mom's eyes were too bright, her words too careful. Yep, she had started early. I caught her at the perfect moment of low resistance before she tipped over into oblivion.

"Good, same old thing. Listen, I have something I need to talk to you about." I took a deep breath and sat down on the ottoman in front of them. "So I got this job offer, and I would really like to take it."

"A job offer? I didn't know you were looking for a job. If you had told me I would have found you something to do in my office." *Yeah, that would be awesome, Dad. Like I don't have to put up with enough of your shit at home.*

"I wasn't really. It just fell into my lap. It seems like a pretty good gig, and it will help a lot with school expenses this fall."

"Oh, are you actually going to college?" The disdain in Dad's voice went right through me. It took all my willpower to keep from wilting or bitch slapping him.

"Yes, Dad, I'm going to college."

"Really? Because it doesn't seem like you've done much on that front. I wasn't sure you were even going to graduate." Throughout my childhood I saw Dad tear Mom apart with little digs here and there—almost a Chinese water torture of insults that kept her constantly thinking she wasn't quite complete. A wife with no confidence was a wife easily controlled. So was a daughter.

I remember once, when I was seven or so, my mom was having a particularly good night. She had even made dinner—a real dinner with side dishes and everything. Dad missed it because of a "late meeting". We were sitting at the dining room table giggling and laughing when he came in. Mom asked where he had been.

"Not shoveling food in my mouth, that's for sure. You know, you can't blame all that weight on having a baby when she's almost a teenager." I don't remember Mom eating even a full meal from that day on.

Every once in a while Dad would turn his attacks on me. When he felt I was maybe getting too strong, too outspoken, or maybe inching away from his control, I would be the recipient of those jabs. Afterward, when I was sullen, or God forbid he caught me crying, he would gasp incredulously. Often it was followed with a shocked, "What's wrong with you? I was just teasing a little."

I wasn't going to fall for it this time—I couldn't. He wasn't going to tell me I was nothing, unacceptable, ever again. My shoulders stiffened. "I'm going to the University of Oklahoma. In Norman. I got my acceptance letter a few weeks ago."

"And how exactly do you plan to pay for that? I'm not footing the bill for out-of-state tuition. Hope you applied at Missouri State because that's the only place you're going. You can live at home and go to college. Save me some money, and your mom won't get lonely. Now, if there's nothing else, I need to go pack. I'm leaving for a trip tomorrow."

Dad pushed himself off the couch and patted me on the head as he walked by. A small reminder that I would stay in my place, he was still in control.

"Honey, you'll have fun at... I mean, maybe you can go to Oklahoma in a year or so... You can always..." Her voice trailed off, her brain grasping for the next word through her vodka haze. There was nothing there. There never was.

"Forget it, Mom. It's no big deal."

"We should go shopping this weekend."

"Yeah, maybe. I'm going to my room."

"Okay, sweetie." She went back to staring at her empty glass.

On the way down the stairs, I realized I hadn't gotten around to telling them about the job with Ken. Not that it mattered. There was no way out—I was never going to escape. It was going to be Mom, Dad and me in this house forever. Drinking, cutting, abusing, and hating each other every single day.

Downstairs, I stood in the hallway between the bedroom and the piano room. Which one tonight? Playing or cutting? Music or blood? If the hall was narrower I could have grabbed both doorknobs at the same time. As it was, my fingertips barely brushed them. I stayed there, my arms extended, grasping for one option or the other, willing my body to lean towards a decision. *I don't care which, just pick one dammit.*

I heard something hit the floor directly above me—Dad must have dropped something. The sound caused me to jump slightly and lose my balance enough to fall towards my bedroom door. It was fate, God, whatever. The decision was made for me. Tonight it would be metal.

It was robotic. Push play on the stereo, take the razors out of the drawer, turn on the small lamp instead of the harsh overhead light, grab the bandages from under the bed—and that's when I saw my duffel bag lying on the closet floor, dirty clothes from the last time I stayed at Maggie's spilling out.

What was keeping me from throwing clothes in there and walking out the door? What could he possibly do to stop me? Lock me in my room? Ground me? Cut me off? Cut me off from what? Him? My mom? Money? I didn't need or want any of it. I grabbed the bag out of the closet.

It held more than just clothing. It held promises. Promises of uninterrupted sleep, someone to care about me, a future. The razor only held promises of more pain. But that pain was my life—it was all I knew. Could I really be something other than a collection of scars and terrors? Something beyond prey? I curled up on my bed, the bag in one hand and the razor in the other.

Sleep and I weren't great friends that night, not that we ever were. By the time the sun started turning the sky a dusky gray, my hands were cramped from holding onto both. I heard the shower start upstairs and knew Dad was getting ready for work. Getting ready to leave. For several days. The only question remaining was what was I going to do about it?

My fist unclenched and the razor rolled out of my hand. It was time to let go.

13.

I shoved handfuls of t-shirts and underwear into my bag, grabbed sheet music without even looking to see what it was, and gathered the cords for my laptop. As I stuffed my phone charger into the side pocket I realized I was really doing it. When I left for school, I had no intention of coming back. Ever.

Mom was stirring upstairs. If I didn't get moving I would have to find a way to sneak my stuff out to the car without her seeing. And I would be late for school. I just needed to hear the front door slam— the sound that meant Dad was gone.

The seconds ticked by. I could hear him in the kitchen. Then walking back to his bedroom. In the living room. What the hell was he doing? If I didn't leave in ten minutes I would need a written excuse to get into class. Shit. Was that the door?

I slung the bag over my shoulder. Where was my backpack? Was it still in my car? I desperately tried to remember if I had carried it in the day before. Had I gone into the piano room last night? Was it in there? It had to be in my car. I had to leave. I had to get out.

I raced up the stairs, my bag banging against the stairwell. *God, please don't let her come out because of the noise.* Shit, where were my keys? In my pocket. They were in my pocket. I could feel them digging into my thigh with each step. My head was sprinting in a thousand different directions.

My hand was on the front door, the finish line was right there—sunlight, freedom, escape.

"Persephone, what are you doing?" Shit. I didn't turn around.

"Going to school, Mom. I'm running late." *Please let me go. No more questions. Just let me go.*

"What's in the bag? It looks like you're running a- oh. I see." *Breathe. All you have to do is breathe. Then open the front door and walk away. You can do this.*

I leaned my head against the door. "Mom, I—"

"No, you need to go. You'll be late for school—you should go. Please take care of yourself."

"I will, Mom." I walked out the door.

The rest of the day was a blur. I'm pretty sure I went to the right classes at the proper times. Not that it mattered. Finals started on Monday, and graduation was the only thing the seniors were interested in talking about.

All I could think about was Mom. I'd abandoned her, left her alone with his wrath. There would be no buffer for her now, no one to distract him from her. What kind of daughter did that make me? Selfish? Hateful? Cruel? Would she ever forgive me for leaving her?

When the last bell rang, I wasn't sure if I could move. Everyone else raced out the doors, pre-summer break energy surging through their veins. I was exhausted. If I could only stay at my desk, I wouldn't have to face any of the decisions waiting for me out there. Should I clean out my locker now or wait until next week? Did I need a date for prom? Would I even go? Where was I going to sleep tonight? Did my mom still love me?

"Persephone, you know class is over, right?" Mrs Hall was smiling at me from the front of the classroom.

"Oh yeah, sorry."

"Are you okay? You seemed, um, preoccupied in class today."

"Yeah, I'm fine. Fight with my boyfriend."

She cocked her head to one side and put on what I'm sure she thought was an inviting, sympathetic smile. "Would you like to talk about it? I remember my first big break-up in high school. It's not easy. But believe me, it's not the end of the world. You have your whole future ahead of you. You will find someone better."

Why is it when adults ask if you want to talk about something they really mean, 'Would you like to sit there while I talk at you? Could you please validate me as a real grown-up, tell me how hip and relatable I am? Could you just stroke my ego a little and let me feel like I've helped you without really having to do anything?'

"Uh huh. I know. He was a douche bag anyway." I could feel it back there, bubbling in my throat, wanting so desperately to come out. *You see, Mrs. Hall, he wanted me to help him start dealing. I guess the cops are on to him, so he needs me to make his regular deliveries. He said they wouldn't suspect someone as sweet-looking as me. I told him I wasn't sure if I could do that. He punched me a few times, but not where the bruises show. He's smart like that.*

I didn't say any of those things. Maybe I'd finally reached my capacity for lying. Maybe that was the last one I had in me, at least for today anyway. I couldn't even look her in the eye anymore.

She giggled, with the *I'm the cool teacher who will let some bad language slide because we're just two buddies talking now* giggle. "Fair enough. Well, if you need anything just let me know. I'm more than a teacher, you know. I really care about my students outside the classroom." *Seriously? What Saved by the Bell episode did you steal that from? If you have to tell your students that then it's not really true.*

"Thanks, I'll keep that in mind. Guess I should get going."

"See you Monday, Persephone."

"Yeah." I gathered my backpack and went into the hallway. It was pretty much empty now. One way led to the front door and my car, where I would have to decide where to go when I exited the parking lot. The other way led to my locker. Prolonging the inevitable, but still inviting.

Taking a step in either direction was too much to handle. I sank back against the wall, staring at my hands. Peeking out from under my sleeves were the tips of almost healed cuts. They were a few weeks old, barely more than scratches now. By the time graduation rolled around in a week, they would fade into the scar tissue already crisscrossing my skin. If I didn't reopen them. My locker could wait. I headed for my car.

Sitting on the hood, smoking a cigarette with all the defiance of an almost-graduated senior, was Maggie. "Dumbass, if they catch you they can suspend you!"

"Yeah, and? I'll miss prom? Not get to walk across the stage with the rest of the idiots at graduation? Do I still get my diploma?"

I shrugged. She had a point. "Um, yeah, I guess. Hell, give me one."

"They're in my bag. I'm not moving."

"Where's your lighter?" Maggie flicked it at me, almost hitting me in the head. "Hey! Watch it! What's wrong with you? You're acting like a very large insect has recently burrowed into your anal cavity."

"Fuck you," Maggie replied.

"Whoa there, skippy pants. What did I do to you?"

"Oh, I can't imagine. Maybe not returning a single damn text or phone call in almost two weeks? Completely disappearing? What kind of fucking friend are you anyway?"

I stood there in the flood of Maggie's anger and expletives, taken completely off-guard. "What the hell are you talking—"

"Please spare me the innocent who-me-look, Persephone." I fumbled to get my phone out of my pocket. "And don't pull the whole 'my phone's not working, it died, it doesn't show any missed calls' bullshit. I've seen you do it to a thousand other people. Delete their calls and then pretend you never got them. Give me more consideration than that, okay? I deserve at least that much."

"No, I wasn't going to—"

"You know, I'm always here when you need me. Phone calls at three in the morning. Canceling dates because you need a place to stay. Convincing my mom you're not a complete freaking loser so she'll let me be friends with you. I'm done, Persephone. We graduate next week. At the end of the summer, I'm leaving for college. You know—college? Are you even going? Forget it, I don't care if you are or not. But I'm not going to be here to watch you wallow anymore. We all have problems—get over yourself, okay? Do yourself a favor and get on with your life, but leave me the hell out of it!"

During her enraged speech I went from contrite to sad to plain old-fashioned pissed off. Who the hell did she think she was? So maybe I had been incommunicado for a week or so. Big deal. It wasn't the end of the world. A few days over the course of a six year friendship? If she was so petty she could walk away over one or two unreturned texts then to hell with her. I didn't need her anyway.

"Fine. What the hell ever. Get your fat ass off my car so I can leave."

Maggie shook her head, looking defeated. "Okay." She slid off and picked up her bag. "It didn't have to be like this, Persephone." She gave me what seemed to be a look of pity. I wanted to punch her.

"Go to hell."

"You know if you would just—"

"I thought you were leaving?" And she did. She walked away.

I needed to drive. I needed to go fast and play loud music. I needed to smoke and yell and feel the rush of knowing one small mistake and my car would run off the road, be smashed to bits, me inside.

A few miles from the school were country roads leading to towns even smaller than mine. I headed in that direction without even thinking. My phone was plugged in, iTunes blaring.

I wasn't even sure what playlist it was on. I didn't care, as long as the music continued to sound loud and angry.

I threw curse words out my window like litter, destroying the peaceful landscape with my filth and waste. My fist pounded my steering wheel and the car filled with haze from one cigarette after the other, even though the window was down.

How dare she? I *was* there for her. We were together all the time on the weekends. I drove her drunk ass home from more parties than I could remember. And what the hell did she mean about canceling dates? She hadn't dated any more than I had! I couldn't remember the last time she even went out with a guy more than a few times.

Well, there was the one guy at the beginning of the year. Mitch, Mike, Marvin? How the hell was I supposed to remember? He was from another school, and I only met him one time. It was a night Mom was drunk when I got home from school, and Dad was supposed to be home from a trip anytime. I texted Maggie two blocks from her house and told her I was staying over.

They were watching a movie when I walked in. I guess she hadn't gotten my text—or didn't read it. Either way, she looked surprised to see me standing in her living room. She untangled herself from him and jumped up. There were awkward introductions. After grunting some sort of response I made a beeline for Maggie's room. I had no desire to be charming for a complete stranger, and Maggie knew that. Twenty minutes later he left, and we didn't mention him again that night.

A few weeks later I asked about him, and she said they weren't seeing each other anymore. She actually looked upset about it. I told her not to worry, he looked like kind of a loser anyway.

Had I told her he couldn't have a ride to the parties we went to over those few weeks? Part of me remembered something like that. And I think I told her I would prefer he not meet us there either. But in all fairness, I knew if Maggie had someone there and I didn't, I would be abandoned. I mean, it's not like she was with me every single night. She had five other nights out of the week to see him, right? Well, at least three nights out of the week. And weren't friends supposed to take precedence over boyfriends? What was the girl equivalent of bros before hos?

She knew when she signed up for the job being my friend wasn't easy. Maggie was the first person who saw my scars for what they were. No amount of lying would deter her. So when she asked why, I didn't even try to cover it up. I spilled everything (well, almost everything), verbally vomiting all over her. Maggie's mom was out that night, hooking up with some new guy, leaving two twelve year old girls to fend for themselves. Something Maggie said was a regular occurrence, like it was no big deal, even though her body language said something entirely different. And for the first time, I saw the reflection of my own screwed up home life in someone else's eyes. We both finally felt some safety in a relationship.

How many nights after that did I text her after midnight, distraught, needing some words of comfort? Not too many. She had been asleep, I knew that. We had a test in science the next day, and I kept her up until two or three in the morning talking. I couldn't remember if either one of us passed, but I didn't think so. It was just one test, after all.

The memories of nights, weekends, skipped classes, and missed parties started piling up in my brain. Yeah, I could keep telling myself Maggie knew what she was getting into, that I gave as much as she did, but was it true? I suddenly didn't think it was.

"Well, shit." I flipped a cigarette butt out the window and looked for a driveway to turn around in. I hated facing the music. I wasn't good at it. "See? This is why I don't like people! This is what happens!" The car didn't answer. "I tried, okay? I tried to be a good friend!" More silence. "Oh shut up!"

I thought about calling Maggie before I showed up at her front door, but why break old habits? Besides, I was afraid she would tell me not to bother, and I didn't want to give her the choice.

14.

Her car was in the driveway. Any other time I would have let myself in, but I figured she deserved more courtesy considering the circumstances. Maggie's eyes were red and puffy when she answered the door. It made me feel even worse. And then I was angry because I felt worse. I fought down the urge to lash out, say horrible things to hurt her even more.

I didn't want to be a predator—see an exposed weakness and exploit it in every way possible. Or pick off the wounded and torture them just because I could. I didn't want to be my father.

"What the hell do you want?"

"Maggie, I'm sorry."

"For what?"

"Seriously?"

"Yes. Tell me what you're sorry for. You don't get off that easy, Persephone."

I was sorry because I was losing one of the only two friends I had in the world. I was sorry because I was hurt. I was sorry because I knew

I'd done something wrong, but I wasn't quite sure what it was. I was sorry because I didn't like feeling this way. I was sorry because I didn't know how to stop feeling this way.

But none of those answers were right. None of them would make it better, and I needed to make it better. I didn't want to lie to Maggie, not anymore. I knew what she wanted to hear. The problem was I didn't know if I would really mean it, or if I would be lying to get myself out of a bad situation. I began small.

"I'm sorry I didn't return any of your calls or texts the past couple of weeks." Did I mean that? Yes, I was sorry about that. If I had taken the time to even say hi back, I wouldn't be in this situation to begin with. Okay, so far so good. "I'm sorry I hurt your feelings." Also true. I was on a roll. "I'm sorry I took you and our friendship for granted. I was in so much pain, I couldn't see beyond what I wanted and needed." Whoa, where did that come from? It felt true. I kept going. "And I'm sorry I lied to you over and over again." Oh shit. Maggie didn't know I'd ever lied to *her*. *Please, please, please say you didn't hear that last part.*

I hurried on. "Can we go inside? Or go for a ride or something? I feel stupid standing in your doorway like this."

"Then feel stupid. I obviously get to feel stupid while my best friend explains all the times she's lied to me."

How in the hell was I going to get out of this one?

"Maggie, I didn't mean it like that. It's just sometimes it's easier to, I don't know. It's like when you know something's going to cause a big drama, so you don't say anything. You know?"

She scoffed. "You? Not want to cause drama? Are you kidding me? You are the *queen* of wreaking havoc! When has consideration for my peace and quiet *ever* stopped you from bursting into my life?"

This was not going well, and she was starting to piss me off again. "Seriously, Maggie, I need a cigarette. Can't we go smoke somewhere?"

"Then smoke. Mom won't be home for hours. Girls' night out." Girls' night out, in Maggie's mom's world, was code for trolling bars for the next likely suspect. She wouldn't come home until some guy was drunk enough to look past the fact she was a middle-aged single mother of a teenager. There was a good chance she wouldn't come home even then. She would stay at his house instead. How many girls' nights out had I been grateful for because it meant I had Maggie and her house all to myself? How many nights had I missed the obvious pain and anger on Maggie's face? I knew the answer. Too many.

"Fine. Come out to my car with me then. Please?"

She shrugged. "Whatever. I need one anyway."

When we got closer to the car, Maggie spied the overstuffed bag in the back seat. "Going somewhere?"

I had come this far—might as well dive in with both feet. "Well, actually, I guess I am."

"What do you mean? Where are you going?"

"There's kind of a funny story about that." Maggie raised her eyebrows, indicating I should tell said funny story. "Let me give you the short version. I got a job taking care of this old guy. It's a full-time, live-in kind of thing. I'm going to work for him through the summer until I leave for school."

"And your parents are okay with that? How did you find this job? Are you even qualified? What's wrong with him? Wait, school? Where are you going? You didn't even tell me you were accepted somewhere."

"Slow down, scooter. I got accepted at OU. I just found out a few days ago. And yes, I'm qualified. It's not like he's dying or anything." But that wasn't really true, was it? I didn't know what was wrong with

Ken. "I stumbled into it through a mutual friend. As far as my parents are concerned, well..." I let the sentence die. What else could I say? It was complicated, and I was worn out. I should have known Maggie wouldn't let it go.

"What do you mean 'well'? They do know you're moving out, right? God, Persephone, please don't tell me you're running away like some little kid!"

"Wouldn't you? I have the chance to get out! I have to take it!"

"Persephone! This is crazy! You're moving in with some old guy, without your parents' permission I might add, and you're acting like it's no big deal. Do you even know this guy? He could be some sick twist that will kill you in your sleep!"

"Listen, Maggie, there's more to the story. It's not like that. I know the guy. I mean, I've been going over there for a while. I've even spent the night there. He's really a good—"

"What the hell, Persephone? God, I don't know anything about you anymore! What do you mean you've been going over there? You are so, so... Jesus, I don't even know the right word. I just can't believe you!"

"Please, Maggie, listen to me. I'll tell you the whole thing. Better yet, why don't you come with me to his house? You can meet him for yourself. I can tell you all about it on the way there. C'mon. You'll really like him." I could see her cracking. It was probably more out of curiosity than forgiveness, but I took what I could get. "Seriously, what else are you going to do? It'll be fun."

"Fine. I'll grab my purse and lock the door. I still think this is a really bad idea, for the record."

"Duly noted."

On the way to Ken's, I filled her in on the missing details—the phone calls from James, the first time I went over to Ken's to read ("Jesus, Persephone! You didn't even know the guy! Are you stupid?"), and the job offer. I left out some of the more intimate details like why I spent the night there and Ken's sister. It wasn't really lying—it was more like a sin of omission. A step in the right direction at least.

When I was done, Maggie stared out the window and stayed silent. I wanted to ask her what she was thinking—if we were okay now—but I was scared of the answer. Once you got on her shit list, it was damn near impossible to get off. My only hope was all the good memories of our friendship would outweigh the crappy ones.

"So here we are." My announcement seemed to startle her. The car had been quiet too long.

"Yep. Well, let's go in and meet this guy."

15.

Ken was dozing in the recliner when we came in. It was a little after five, and I wondered how long he had been asleep. Had he been waiting on me? Great, my first day 'on the job', and I was already screwing things up.

"Ken, it's me. Wake up." I gently tapped his shoulder, and he came awake with a start and his fists clenched.

"Oh, Persephone, it's you. Sorry, I was just resting."

"That's okay. I hope it's alright, I brought a friend with me. She wanted to meet you." It made him sound like an exhibit at a carnival sideshow.

"No, that's fine. Come on in." He struggled to get out the chair, and I put out my arm to help steady him. His weight wasn't as hard to hold as I thought it would be. When had he gotten so thin and why hadn't I noticed before now?

Maggie was all but huddled in the entryway. I realized the one thing I hadn't told her about was the sheer force of Ken's presence. Sure, he scared the crap out of me the first time we met, but that seemed so long ago. He was just Ken now. I wanted to tell her it was okay, he wasn't nearly as scary as he looked. Ken beat me to it.

"Don't worry, I won't bite. I'm Ken. And you are?" He held out his hand, and Maggie stepped forward.

"I'm Maggie," she whispered, letting her hand be swallowed in his.

He turned to me. "She's just as quiet as you were. How about that."

"She's not usually. Maggie, say something."

"It's nice to meet you, sir." I giggled at how similar she sounded to me the first time I met Ken.

"Why don't you girls come in and sit down? Would you like something to drink?" Maggie shook her head, obviously still too intimidated to say much. "Persephone, would you mind getting me some tea? I think I would like to sit back down."

"Yeah, sure. Are you okay?"

"Fine, fine." He waved his hand, dismissing me. I was hurt by the gesture but more concerned about the color, or lack thereof in his face. Once again, I wondered when all of this had happened. When did he start looking so old?

I returned with his tea to find him still trying to draw Maggie out. "So are you off to school as well this fall?"

"Yes, sir."

"Maggie's going to MU. She's really smart and got an almost perfect on her ACT. All kinds of scholarships, right, Maggie?" I bragged. She only nodded.

"Well, good for you. What will you study there?"

She cleared her throat. "Pre-med. I'm going into medical research. I'm going to cure MS."

This caught my attention. It was the first time I'd heard about this plan. I always knew she wanted to go into medicine, but I had no idea about the research. What the hell was MS? And more importantly, why the hell did she want to cure it?

"That certainly sounds ambitious." Ken was obviously impressed. "What made you choose that?"

Maggie glanced in my direction, hesitating before answering. "A friend of mine, his dad has multiple sclerosis." *What the hell? What friend?* My dad was, as much as I wished it wasn't the case, in perfect health. "I mean, this guy I used to date, Mickey, his dad has it."

Mickey! That was his name! Did I remember Maggie telling me about his dad? Did I remember Maggie telling me anything, period? Not really. I did, however, remember alternating between making fun of his name and his stereotypical Irish appearance. Jesus.

"There was this one time I was at his house and Mick's dad had an attack. They call it an episode. Anyway, his legs started to spasm, and he collapsed. Mick had to carry him to bed like a baby. Mick's a big guy, but so is his dad. It was hard to watch, but it was kind of beautiful, too, you know? It's just the two of them. His mom left a few months after his dad was diagnosed. It's really hard on them. We don't really see each other much anymore. I mean, I haven't seen him at all. We texted a few times, but, you know." She shrugged, trying to be casual about something that obviously meant a lot to her. "His dad was getting worse, and Mick spends a lot of his time taking care of him. And I..." She looked me in the eye and said, "I had my own obligations to take care of."

Heart meet floor. And here's a curb stomp to finish the job. I reached for her hand. "Maggie, I'm so sorry. I had no idea."

She let me briefly hold her fingers before putting her hand back in her lap.

"I know."

I guess things weren't all better yet. Guilt, shame and anger collided in one sickening pool in my stomach. She should have told me! We were together all the time! At any point she could have said, "Hey, Persephone, you know that guy I'm dating? Yeah, I really like him, and his dad's sick, and I'm worried." I would have listened. I would have been there for her. I would have told her to go spend time with him. It wasn't my fault she never said anything! But was that true? Really?

Silence joined us in the living room, sidling up and whispering words of regret, sadness and anger into my ears. *You weren't there for her. You are a bad friend. No, it's worse than that. You're a bad person. You are selfish and cruel. How many cuts will it take to make this better? How much blood are you willing to sacrifice this time?*

Ken finally broke through. "Alright girls, it's getting close to dinner time. We're going to order pizza. I prefer pepperoni from Imo's. If you would like something different, feel free to order another for yourselves. If not, I think an extra-large should feed us all. Persephone, there is cash in the coffee can on the kitchen counter. I think I will take a short nap. Please wake me up when it gets here."

"Okay. Everything okay?"

He nodded, pushing himself out of his chair, but didn't say anything.

"Ken?"

"I'm fine, Persephone."

I was once again struck by his sudden change in mood and chilly tone. Did he realize *I* was the obligation Maggie was talking about? Was he angry? Disappointed? I needed so desperately for him to turn around and smile. Pat me on the head. Anything to let me know everything was okay. But he left the room and a few moments later I heard his door shut.

"So that's Ken, huh? He's nice, I guess. Listen, I don't think I'll stick around for the pizza thing. Can you take me home?" *Fine, you can leave me, too. What the hell do I care? Screw you both.*

"Yeah, I guess so. I can just pick up the pizza, I guess." *And razors. Oh, and bandages.*

"I just, you know, want to be at my house and stuff. No offense."

"Yeah, no, I get it." *You could ask her to stay. She doesn't know you need her unless you tell her.*

"Okay, well." *She might need you, too.*

"I'll get my keys." *She doesn't need someone like you. Someone who cuts her own body and lies and runs away and uses people. No one needs you. And no one wants you.* I stood in the living room entryway, waiting for some other voice to tell me something different.

"Persephone?" Maggie was getting impatient.

"Maggie, would you please stay? I know you want to go home. I know I shouldn't ask. And I will take you home if you want me to. But could you just stay for a little while? I feel so lost."

Maggie knelt down on the floor beside me and wrapped her arms around me. "Me too, but we're going to be okay."

I tried to nod but ended up head butting her in the chin instead. It was the moment we needed to break through. Tears and pain were replaced by laughter and acceptance. It was time to order pizza.

His room was dark save for a small, dim lamp on the nightstand—a nightstand covered in prescription bottles. *Take two as needed for pain. Take as needed. Take (4) four 3 times a day with food. Take as needed for sleep. Take 2 once a day.* I kept picking up bottles. What were they all for? Again, I knew I didn't want the answer to my question. I could pretend I had never seen them. I had spent my life convincing myself things weren't true—weren't really happening. I could make this go away, too.

"Ken?" I whispered. "Ken?" His hand flew from his side and locked around my wrist. His eyes were open and staring at me, unknowing and uncaring. It'd never occurred to me that maybe I wasn't the only one with nightmares.

"Ow! Ken! Let go!" I tried to pull free, giving myself an Indian burn in the process. "*Ken! Please!*" The cloud seemed to lift and he released my arm. I backed away, not knowing if I should run or comfort him.

"Persephone! I'm sorry. It's okay. Sometimes I get confused."

"Ken, what's wrong with you?" I didn't just mean what caused him to come out of sleep fighting. Or what made him need the pharmacy on his nightstand. I wanted to know what made him sit for hours holding a picture of his sister and crying. And how he had reached almost the end of his life with only a screwed up teenager and an old Marine buddy to care about him.

"It's bad memories, Persephone. Everyone has them. Some are worse than others."

"I know."

"I'm sorry if I frightened you."

"It's okay. The pizza is here." I couldn't look him in the eye. I *was* scared, but not for the reasons he thought. I was terrified to realize everyone I knew and loved was damaged, flawed beyond repair. There was no pursuit of happiness—just a constant battle to keep the worst of the demons at bay.

"Alright."

Comments about the pizza and which kind was our favorite covered up the fact none of us were really talking. At least not about anything that mattered. Not about all the things we could and should have been talking about. All the things none of us *wanted* to talk about.

When the last bit of crust had been eaten and the box shoved in the trash can, we had no choice but to stare at one another.

Ken finally claimed exhaustion and went to bed. Despite his earlier nap, he did look worn out. When we heard his door shut, Maggie asked if I would take her home.

We were in the car for at least five minutes before either one of us spoke. Maggie was the one to break the silence.

"You know, Persephone, I think this is all going to work out. I like Ken." I reached over to hold her hand.

"I hope you're right, Maggie. I really do."

We pulled into her driveway. "Just have a little faith. Sometimes things actually do go right, you know?"

"Yeah, I guess. I mean, we're still friends right?" I tried to sound casual about it, but there was a break in my voice.

"Always, Persephone, always."

I waited to make sure she got into her house okay. On my way back to Ken's I realized my phone had been silent all night—Mom hadn't called or texted. I told myself not to worry about what she was doing all by herself, but it was easier said than done.

16.

Mom finally called while I was driving to school the next morning. I hadn't even thought about lighting a cigarette until I saw her name on the screen. I fumbled to light one and answer at the same time.

"Hi, Mom."

"Good morning, sweetheart. I was calling to check in, see if you might be coming home tonight. Dad's gone on a trip for the next few days." She sounded so small and defeated. I didn't want to hear her voice anymore. I didn't want her to need me like this.

"Maybe, Mom. I have some errands and stuff to do after school. Maybe I'll come by later?"

"That would be good, Persephone. I love you." I felt another hook attaching itself to me, dragging me back to her, my dad—to destruction.

"K, Mom. Bye." I flicked the cigarette out the window as I pulled into a parking space. I only had a few days left. Who cared about school policy?

Maggie and I walked in together. There was a brief, awkward silence, but things were better. When we saw each other in the hallways, we exchanged our private this-is-a-freaking-joke smiles. I got a text from her fourth period expressing her dismay at still being in class and asking if I wanted to grab coffee after school. I told her I had to run some errands for Ken, but she was welcome to come along. We could grab a Dirty White Boy (the ultimate coffee drink) from Classic Rock while we were out. My treat. I got a smiley face back.

She was perching on my car, much like the day before, but today she was smiling, face turned to the sun—the perfect picture of a contented teen, ready to grab the world by the horns. It was funny how deceptive appearances could be.

"Hey, bub," I greeted her.

"What are we shopping for?"

"Food and new sheets. Really fun stuff."

"Most definitely." We laughed and got in the car. Maggie cranked up the radio, Eminem rattling the windshield. It felt good to have my friend back.

We giggled and criticized various bed sets for the next hour, finally picking a bright tie-dyed one with a matching comforter. I thought Ken would like it. Or at least it would make him smile.

At the grocery store, we meticulously followed Ken's list. He had written brand names and quantities next to each item. It was impressive.

"You know, this stuff is going to get hot if I take you back to your car before I drop it at Ken's house. Do you mind running over there first?"

"No that's fine. Mom actually came home last night. Guess she couldn't reel in a new victim. Anyway, she started in on me about my outfit for graduation and my reception. She wants to go shopping, and I'm doing everything I can to not do that. She has shitty taste in clothes. Where are you having your reception?"

"Uh, I don't know. I guess I'm not having one."

"Are you serious? Your mom hasn't planned anything?"

"No. I think Dad will be out of town on a trip. It's really no big deal." And it wasn't. The normal milestones of high school meant something vastly different to me than to my peers. Graduation wasn't a celebration. It was a day to get through, another step closer to freedom.

I wasn't having a reception because there wasn't anyone to invite. My dad had colleagues not friends. My mom's social circle didn't extend beyond Jim, Jack, and Jose. She did have a sister somewhere in South Dakota, but they rarely spoke.

My aunt had come to visit when I was little. It was for my grandparents' funeral. Car crash on a dream trip to New York. All I could remember was a shouting match between my aunt and my father. Dad called his sister a meddlesome bitch, and she had never come back. I had cousins I only knew through pictures on Christmas cards.

And the last thing I wanted was a present from my father.

"What about Project Graduation? Did you buy your ticket yet?"

It hadn't crossed my mind.

"I don't think I'm going to go." Locked in for the entire night with hundreds of people I had no desire to spend more than thirty minutes with under normal circumstances? A vision of school board-approved activities, music, and snacks filled my head. I shuddered. No thank you.

"Come on, Persephone! Don't make me go alone! I know you're not going to prom. Don't miss this, too!" It was true. I had turned down three guys for prom, and word got out to not even bother. I had officially solidified my position as resident, bitchy ice queen. It had only taken four years of diligent, daily effort. Good to know the hard work had paid off.

"Why don't you not go, and we'll hang out together that night?" I suggested.

"No! I know you're not into all of this, and I'm really not either, but come on! We only get to graduate high school once. It's just one night. Please Persephone!" I could feel my resolve wavering. It wasn't because I was getting all sentimental and gushy. It was because it was Maggie asking. And I owed her. She had missed a lot because of me. I needed to do this for her.

"Fine. I will get my freaking ticket tomorrow, okay?" She actually squealed and clapped her hands. I laughed.

We dropped off groceries and made my bed with the new sheets. I was right, they made Ken smile. I took Maggie home. She chirped happily the whole way there about nothing in particular. It was nice to hear her sound like Maggie again.

Later that night, as I curled into my new bed for the first time, I realized I never went to see Mom. I hadn't even called.

17.

It was the last Friday the seniors would ever grace the halls of the high school, and it was chaotic. Teachers tried their best to keep us in line and somewhat out of trouble. It didn't work. A box of miniature bouncing balls was released into the student center in between morning classes. The fountain was filled with dish soap and smoke bombs went off in one of the girls' bathrooms.

When we were finally released, I rushed out to my car, determined to get to Mom's as soon as possible. I felt bad for not seeing her the night before.

The house was dark and silent when I walked in. "Mom? Are you here?" No answer. I walked down the hallway towards her bedroom. The door was shut. I knocked. "Mom?"

The drapes were pulled and the lights were out. Mom was curled up in the corner of her bed with an empty bottle of vodka on the nightstand. There was no glass. She was drinking straight out the bottle now. My stomach was a rock sitting in the middle of my internal organs.

Everything came crashing down around me. The weight of my family, my home, my life pounded on my shoulders and head. How did I think I could leave? Who was going to take care of her now? I couldn't do much for her, but at least I could keep her from finally disappearing into a bottle. It would only get worse when Dad got home and discovered I was gone. Without me there, all of his attention and energy would be focused completely on her. What would she do then? How long before she broke?

"Mom." I nudged her shoulder. "Mom, it's me. I'm home."

Her eyes struggled to open and she looked at me, confused. "You were supposed to be here yesterday."

"I know. I'm sorry. I got caught up doing other things, and I ran out of time. I should have called."

"I wasn't expecting you tonight." *Well no shit. You were probably almost sober last night.*

"Yeah, well here I am." She rubbed her eyes and tried to sit up. Her hair was sticking out at crazy angles and there were remnants of yesterday's make-up smeared across her face. It was like watching *Whatever Happened to Baby Jane* rise from my mother's bed.

"Good. I'm so glad to see you. My head is throbbing. Would you mind getting me some aspirin and a glass of water?"

"Sure, Mom. Of course I will." I patted her hand. *Of course I will take care of you, Mom. I will always take care of you. And one day, maybe you will take care of me, too. It's okay. I know right now you can't. But maybe one day...*

I rummaged around for some Tylenol wondering how I was going to tell Ken I couldn't do it. I couldn't leave her. He would understand, right? And Maggie would be okay with me not going to Project Graduation. This was a good place actually to go ahead and end our friendship. She would be leaving for college in a few months and would never need to look back. Who kept friends their entire life anyway?

I sat back down on the edge of her bed. "Here, Mom. Sit up."

"Oh thank you, sweetie. You know, your dad is coming back home tomorrow. It was a short trip."

"Okay."

"Don't you think you should be here when he gets back? I mean, don't you think that would be better for everyone?" For the first time she looked me straight in the eye, clear and focused. I didn't understand. How could she possibly think things would be better for me?

"For everyone, Mom? Really?"

"Sweetheart, your dad knows you're supposed to be grounded. And I know you think you left this house for good. But enough's enough. You've proven your point. Now come back home so everything can be okay. Everything can go back to normal." Mom patted my cheek and lay back down, snuggling into her pillow. "Would you mind finding yourself something for dinner? I just don't feel very good right now."

She knows! Oh my God, she knows! I felt sick. Maybe she didn't know it all, but Mom knew her life was easier when I was there—when I could help absorb his abuse. And when she weighed my life out over hers, she deemed hers more valuable. Everything shattered.

"Yeah, I'll do that."

"You're such a good girl." And with that her eyes closed. I didn't know if she had fallen asleep or passed out. How much had she had to drink today? Was that bottle from last night or this afternoon?

You can't afford to care anymore. Run.

And I did.

Ken was waiting for me in the living room when I got there. "Hey, kiddo. I was starting to get worried about you."

"I'm sorry. I had to go by and see my mom after school."

"That's okay. Everything alright at home?"

"Sure, just needed to check in on her. Dad's gone on a trip."

"That's not what I meant. Don't you think it's time we talk about what's going on at your home?" *Oh Jesus, why? Why do we need to do this now? Why do we need to do this ever?*

"Nothing's going on at home. My relationship with my parents is just…complicated." I couldn't look him in the eye. Had I ever outright lied to him? I wasn't really lying then—it was an oversimplification.

"Persephone, let's get something perfectly clear before we go any further. You need to be here as much, if not more, than I need you here." I opened my mouth to say something, and he held up his hand. There was no arguing with that gesture. "Let me finish. I may be old, and my eyesight may not be what it used to be, but I'm not stupid. There is a reason you would rather be here than at home or out with your friends. Or friend, since you only have one that I know of." *Well, that's kind of cold.* "There is also a reason you have scars all over your arms."

I instinctively crossed them over my chest, trying to hide them. How in the hell had he seen them? I had been so careful!

He shook his head. "That doesn't do you any good, Persephone. Is everyone in your life blind? Do your parents wilfully ignore them? Never mind. The answer is painfully, horribly obvious." He sounded angry. His words were like sandpaper over raw skin. I didn't want to hear anymore. I had to say something—anything—to make him stop.

"Ken, listen, it was something stupid I did. I don't really—"

"Stop. Just stop. I don't know what's going on, and I'm not entirely sure I want to. What I do know is I care about you. If your parents aren't going to take care of you, I will. Do you understand?"

You don't deserve this. You know that, right? He may think he cares about you, but if he knew—if he knew everything—he wouldn't want to have anything to do with you.

"Persephone, are you listening to me?" I couldn't look up. I couldn't speak. "Persephone?"

"Ken, I... I don't think you understand." Then the sobs came, uncontrollable and violent. Each breath hurt and my face contorted in pain. Ken crossed the room to wrap his arms around me.

"Shhh. It's going to be okay. I promise. Everything is going to be okay." He smoothed my hair with his hand, trying to calm me down. "Good Lord, what have they done to you?" I don't think he was actually looking for an answer. Or maybe he was, but it wasn't one I could give him right then. All I could do was cry and let myself be soothed.

Ken kissed me on top of my head. "I didn't think there was much point to my life anymore. I didn't think there were more enemies to be fought. I guess I was wrong."

The next morning, I woke up before Ken did. I cracked open his door to check on him, and heard him snoring. It was only seven-thirty, but I thought he would like to wake up to the smell of bacon and coffee. I found the skillet and coffee filters and set to work. It felt nice to be making breakfast to make someone happy as opposed to coaxing a drunk parent out of bed.

"Well, good morning. What a pleasant surprise. Did you sleep well?" Ken asked, as he walked into the kitchen, his robe cinched around flannel pajamas and slippers on his feet.

"I did, thank you. And you?"

"Yes, thank you."

We ate our breakfast in companionable silence. The bacon was a little overdone, but Ken didn't seem to mind. His appetite was better.

"So what do you want to do today?" I asked when our plates were empty.

"I was thinking we could start a new book today, if you would like. And at some point there are a couple of errands I need you to run for me."

"Sure. I'm going to shower real quick, if that's okay and then tackle the breakfast mess. We can read after that."

"Of course. The bathroom across the hall from your room is all yours. There are clean towels in the cabinet under the sink. I'll shower after you're done."

"Great."

While I was braiding my hair, my scars flashed a few times in the mirror, but I did my best to ignore them. I didn't want to think about them—I didn't want to remember they were there. Not today.

Maggie sent a text while I was cleaning up the kitchen. "Prom tonight. Not going. I think I'm going to go see Mickey instead. Do you want to hang out tomorrow?" *Mickey, huh? Good for you, Mags.*

"Sure. Tell Mickey I say hi. On second thought, don't. He probably doesn't have fond memories of me."

"Lol. I'll tell him. I'll give you a shout tomorrow."

"Cool."

There were no other missed calls or texts. Not that I expected to hear from Mom this early in the morning. With Dad not due home until sometime early evening, she wouldn't even make an effort to get out of bed until after three.

Ken still wasn't out when I was done with the kitchen, so I wandered into the living room. There were so many books. Which one was he going to choose? As if on cue, I heard his voice behind me.

"Have you read anything by Kurt Vonnegut?"

"Uh, I know some of his books have been banned? I'm sorry, I'm not much of a reader."

"It's okay. You will be. Get *Slaughterhouse-Five* off the shelf. It's a quick read. You'll like it." We made it through the first chapter before Ken started to doze off.

"Do you want me to stop?"

"Maybe so. I guess I didn't sleep as well as I thought I did." He tried to smile. "You could go run those errands if you wanted to. I'll get a little rest."

"Of course."

"The list and money are on the table in the entryway. It should be fairly self-explanatory."

"Are you sure you're okay?"

"Of course. I'm just old, Persephone. It happens."

"So it goes." That made him chuckle.

I called James as I pulled out of the driveway. We hadn't spoken in a few days, and I had no idea how much he knew of what was going on.

"Well, hey there, sweet pea. How are you and the old man gettin' along?" The sound of his voice made everything feel more solid.

"Oh you know, he's a pretty tough guy to handle, but I think I'm holding my own."

"I bet you are." He chuckled. There were a few moments of silence, and I knew James was giving me the chance to bring it up first.

"So, I guess Ken has probably told you about the job offer."

"Well yes, him and me discussed it. I thought it was a fine idea. I can't think of two better people to be takin' care of each other. Are you all settled in?"

"Yeah, it's nice. I play the piano, too." *Apropos of nothing.*

"That's what I heard. I'm sure he likes hearing it again. How's he doing?"

"Good! Well, I mean, he seems to be tired a lot lately and I can't get him to eat much, although he did eat a pretty good breakfast. But he's doing really good. We started a new book today. And James, I promise I won't be any trouble for him. I promise."

"I know you won't, sweet pea. You two need each other, and nothing more needs to be said about it, okay?"

"Okay."

"Alright. Well you take care, and give me a holler if you need anything. We'll talk again soon."

"Sounds good. Bye, James."

"Bye now."

Ken needed shaving cream and aspirin from the drug store and a list of books picked up from Barnes & Noble. There was a Stephen King book about the assassination of JFK that looked interesting. I bought a latte and sat down in the little café to read a few pages before heading back. It was as weird as it was relaxing. I wasn't escaping. I wasn't trying to distract myself. I wasn't anything except being. It wasn't until I pulled into the driveway I realized not only had I not thought about cutting, I also hadn't smoked in two days. *Watch it kid, you might be getting happy.* That made me smile.

The rest of the weekend was lazy and uneventful. We made it through half of *Slaughterhouse-Five*, and Ken promised we would start on the Stephen King book next, as long as I promised not to read any more first. Maggie and I hung out at our favorite coffee shop while she told me all about her evening with Mickey and his dad. She hinted there was a chance of them getting back together, even though Mickey would be staying in Springfield for college and she would be three hours away. Ken taught me a game called Shut the Box. It was kind of mindless but fun. We played for pennies.

My phone didn't ring. I was surprised, but mostly relieved. Maybe, just maybe.

18.

Monday morning dawned clear and bright. Three days of school left. Graduation on Saturday afternoon. I sailed through my finals and even chatted with a few classmates. Like, engaged in genuine small talk about the prom. I may have even seemed interested, without a hint of sarcasm. There were a few times I was tempted to sneak into the bathroom, look in the mirror and make sure it was really me looking back.

Maggie and I met at the front door after the last bell. "Hey, killer. Don't you look like the cat that ate the canary? Did you make a cheerleader cry or something?"

"I'm allowed to just be in a good mood, right?"

"Sure. Of course you're allowed. But are you capable? Hey, I'm just kidding! It's good to see you smile! Did you get your Project Graduation ticket yet?"

I patted my purse. "Right here, baby. All purchased and ready for a night of frivolity and shallow fun with a group of people I hope never to see again in my life. If you ask me, fifteen dollars well spent."

"Smartass. Well, hey, I'm running over to Mick's for a while. I figured you would be over at Ken's. Want to try to do something tomorrow?" I fought down the urge to tell her I wanted to do something today or not at all. It was petty and spiteful—two things I was trying very hard to get rid of.

"Yeah, great. Have fun with Mickey!" I waved as she veered off in the other direction towards her car.

On the way home, I thought about the Alfredo sauce recipe I had found online during class earlier. I was anxious to try it out and hoped Ken was up for pasta. I was pretty sure there was a box of frozen cheese bread I could make to go with it. Maybe I would run to the store and get a pie or something for dessert. Maybe the Mrs Smith's Reese's Peanut Butter pie. That would make him happy.

These were the thoughts running through my head when I turned onto Ken's street. When I saw my father's car sitting in his driveway, my stomach twisted in on itself. I gagged, feeling the bagel and cream cheese fighting its way out. I barely got the car slowed and the door open before it tumbled out of my mouth and splashed onto the street. What was he doing here? How had he found me? I knew the answer almost before the question had formed in my head. Fucking phone tracker.

There was nowhere left to run. There was no safe place. I was out of options. He had taken everything from me. Pure hatred and rage caused my cheeks to flame. I could feel the heat of it in every pore. I wanted to scream. I wanted to beat someone. I wanted blood. I wanted to stop feeling like my body and mind were exploding and shrinking at the same time. I wanted anything but to go inside, but it was my only option.

The front door was unlocked, which was good. I didn't think I could focus enough to get my key in the hole. I stood on the threshold, not sure what to do next. I could hear the murmuring of voices in the living room. What was he saying? What was he telling Ken about me?

"Persephone, I assume that's you. Please come in here." Ken's voice drew me in. My natural instinct was to obey.

Dad was sitting in my chair (*asshole, that doesn't belong to you. That's mine*), arms resting on his knees, leaning forward. Whatever the discussion was, it was obviously intense. I hovered on the edge of the living room.

"Your dad was just telling me a few things about you, Persephone. Things he thought I should know. Perhaps you should repeat them for your daughter, Mr Daniels." Ken's face was grim. I leaned against the wall and stared at the floor, ashamed and embarrassed. I couldn't face him. I knew whatever my dad had told him, it was something to make Ken not want me anymore. Something that would make sure I went back home. I almost turned around to go get my bags from my room.

"Well, Persephone, since you spend so much time here, I thought this nice gentleman should know what kind of person you are exactly. For instance, I have noticed lately that some of my Xanax have gone missing." He turned to Ken. "I have a slight anxiety issue. The stress of work and having a teenager in this day and age. I rarely take them. As a matter of fact, I prefer to leave the bottle at home when I travel and only take a few with me. When I left for this trip there were fifteen in the bottle. Now there are only six. Do you have any prescriptions in the house? Have you checked them lately?"

Ken shook his head. I could feel the tears burning in the rims of my eyes. I had never touched his pills, but why would Ken believe that? Why would anyone believe me over a grown man? Over my father?

"She is also an adroit liar, aren't you, Persephone?"

I nodded. What was the point in not being truthful now?

"You should hear some of the stories she makes up. I worry sometimes her only options for a career are criminal or writer. Neither of which are exactly promising, wouldn't you agree?" Dad gave Ken the we're-in-this-together-wink. "So I think it would be best if Persephone went and got her things, so I can take her home. Her mom and I will come back and get her car tomorrow."

Why did my own father hate me so much? He was supposed to love and cherish me. Treat me like a princess and walk me down the aisle. Daddies are supposed to protect their little girls. Nothing in my brain could make it okay.

Ken gripped the arms of his recliner and sat up straight.

"Mr Daniels, I appreciate you taking the time to tell me all of this. If I had known you felt like this, Persephone and I would have had a much different conversation before she came to stay here." Dad leaned back in his chair, satisfied. His toy would be home by dinner.

"I will go get my stuff."

"No, Persephone, you will stand here and listen to what I have to say. And you will pick your head up." When I looked at him, Ken had a single tear running down his cheek. Oh god, I had hurt him. He'd trusted me, taken care of me, and I broke his heart. Everything was numb.

"Now let me tell you what I know about Persephone. I know that three months ago she had no plans for her future and no hope of having one. I know she felt alone and scared. I know she was rude and defeated. I know she has now taken it upon herself to only get accepted to college but also secure the funding she needs to go to that college. I know Persephone is beginning to see that life does still hold some joy. And she knows she is no longer alone.

"What I also know, Mr Daniels, is that while you may be her father I will not let you destroy everything Persephone has built for herself. With all due respect, which I expect is very little, I must insist you leave my home immediately. And you will be leaving without Persephone. She is staying here."

The anger emanating from both men was palpable. It was crushing me. Dad stood, his bottom lip disappearing, the explosion imminent.

"Listen, you son of a bitch, I don't care who the hell you think you are or what you think you know, but that is *my* daughter. I—"

Ken sprang from his chair and crossed the room in two steps. He was at least three inches taller than my father, and in that moment I could see the young man Ken once was. The Marine he would always be.

"You will do nothing but leave this house. Persephone is not the only person in this room I know. I know you, too. I know more about you than I ever wanted to. You may have the two women in your life terrified of you, but you don't scare me. I may be old, but I can still handle a piece of garbage like you. I am a United States Marine, sir, and I will kick your ass. Now get the hell out of here." The last sentence was punctuated with a forceful poke to Dad's chest.

"I will leave because she isn't worth all of this. You can keep her." On his way out, he paused and whispered, "You will come home, Persephone. You're my little girl." When I heard the door slam, I crumpled to the floor and Ken sank into his chair.

"Persephone, are you okay?" I nodded and realized he couldn't see me. I couldn't get my mouth to work, though. "Persephone?" I managed to crawl around the corner to the front of his chair. I laid my head on his knee and felt him pat the top of my head. His hand rested there.

"Everything's going to be alright. It's going to be okay."

"No, it's not. You don't understand. He isn't going to go away. He'll be back. He always comes back."

"Persephone, he's done. He's a bully. A bully and a coward. And a coward will never fight when it is easier to run away."

I don't know how long we sat there like that, but eventually we both agreed we were hungry. I made grilled cheese and soup, the recipe for Alfredo sauce forgotten. Ken ate in his chair, a tray in his lap. I sat on the floor in front of him. Neither of us spoke. I cleaned up the plates and bowls afterwards. As I was scrubbing the frying pan, I heard Ken come into the kitchen.

"Persephone, I need you to listen to what I am about to say and believe me." I turned around to face him. "You are safe here. I won't let him hurt you ever again. Do you understand me?"

"Yes, sir."

"Do you believe me?"

"Yes, sir."

And the funny thing was I did.

19.

On Wednesday afternoon, Maggie and I walked out of our high school for the last time with the whooping and hollering of our classmates surrounding us. We exchanged high fives with classmates and chatted about graduation on Saturday—who was having a reception before and who after and which ones we should try to go to. Yearbooks were passed around for last minute signatures. Mine stayed tucked in my bag. I didn't want to know what my classmates had to say about me. I was pretty sure they felt the same way.

When we finally made it to our cars, Maggie and I were both worn out—way too much social interaction crammed into a short amount of time.

"Are you coming by the house Saturday? You can bring Ken if you want." Maggie's mom was hosting a brunch before the ceremony. Maggie had already threatened a lifetime of silence if I didn't come help her deal with the crush of family and her mother's friends.

"Yeah, of course. Wouldn't miss it for the world."

"Thanks, Persephone. Hey, are you sure your parents aren't doing anything for you? I mean, it's your high school graduation and I know you guys aren't really…" As many issues as Maggie had with her mom she still could not comprehend a parent simply walking away from their child. Completely giving up.

"I'm sure. It's no big deal, Maggie, I promise. I have you and Ken. It's fine. I wouldn't want them there anyway. I want to be happy on Saturday." I plastered on what I hoped was a convincing smile and gave her a hug.

"I'll see you Saturday, okay?"

"Alrighty. Oh, did I tell you Mick is going to be there?"

"Awesome! Can't wait to see him again."

One more hug and we parted ways. In my car, I let my mind go where I had refused to let it over the past two days. I had not heard from Dad again. For all I knew, he was back out on the road. Mom had not called either. One filled me with hope. The other was crushing. Would she really let me go without a backwards glance? Was the fear of him greater than her love for me? Or worse, was her apathy? I didn't even know if she was coming to my graduation or not. I told myself it didn't matter. Myself didn't believe me.

There was a car parked in Ken's driveway—a dark sedan with out-of-state plates. My first thought was Dad sent someone to arrest me—a juvenile officer to bring in the big, bad, non-existent Xanax thief. My second thought was something had happened to Ken. I barely had the car in park before I was out and running to the front door.

"Ken? Ken? Are you okay?" I skidded to a halt in the living room when I saw someone sitting in my rocking chair. He was older and grayer, wearing a flannel shirt and jeans instead of Marine dress. And there was a small paunch in front that wasn't there before, but there was no mistaking him. Sitting across from Ken was James.

I couldn't move. I couldn't speak. They were both here, right in front of me. My two warriors, heroes. It was too much for my mind to process and my heart to take.

"Well, there she is. Miss Persephone, I presume?" James stood and held out his arms. I nodded and walked to him. "It's so nice to meet ya, sweet pea."

"Uh huh." I meant to say more, I really did. I meant to hold it together. I meant to be calm and composed. I meant to sound human. None of that happened. I snuffled and snotted against his shirt as he patted my back and tried to soothe me.

"It's okay, hon. It's all okay." It seemed like people were telling me that a lot lately. Eventually maybe I would believe them.

James held me out at arm's length and grinned. "Why don't you go wash your face? I'm taking you and this old coot out for dinner. I assume there's some decent barbecue somewhere in these parts." He hitched his thumbs through his belt loops and puffed out his chest, the perfect imitation of a small town, southern sheriff. I expected him to turn his head to the side and spit at any moment.

"There's a place over near my school. I've never been in it, but some of the football players swear by it. They go over there all the time before games. Um, City Butcher, I think?"

"Well then that's the place. Ken, you ready to take this girl out on the town?"

I glanced over my shoulder at him. He looked tired but content. There had been a lot of activity in his life lately. Maybe he needed to rest. "You know, I could just go pick something up and bring it back. They do carry-out, too."

"No, no, no. It's not often I have my two favorite people in the same place. We all deserve a night out. James, you okay with driving? Persephone has a clown car."

James' laugh filled every corner of the house and warmed me down to my toes. "Of course I will! Now let's get going!" James pulled his USMC Vietnam Vet cap on and herded us towards the door.

City Butcher was packed. There was a party of five (Mom, Dad and three rambunctious kids) in front of us waiting for a table as well. I contemplated the feasibility of tripping them as they ran in circles around their parents' legs. Would the ensuing injured crying be worse than the ear-piercing squealing?

Before I could test my hypothesis, the hostess came back and motioned to the dad. "You're table is ready, sir."

He turned and looked at us, and replied, "No, they were here first." The wife grinned and whispered something in the ears of her brood.

The oldest of the three (he may have been six) stepped in front of James and stuck out his hand. "Thank you for serving, sir. Daddy says my grandpa was in that war, too. Are you her grandpa?"

"You are quite welcome, young man. And yes, she belongs to me." The little boy nodded. Everything was just as it should have been in his world. The hostess shrugged, completely indifferent to the entire exchange.

As we passed, I patted the father on the arm and whispered thank you. He only nodded, lost in memories of his own father. Maybe wishing he had more.

An annoyingly cheerful waitress came over to take our order. James didn't even allow us to open the menu. "We need three teas. Two sweet and one unsweet. Persephone, I will not let him corrupt you into drinking that heathen unsweet stuff. It just ain't proper. We'll take a slab of ribs, a large side of slaw and a large side of beans. And three plates. Can you get that for us, darlin'?" It didn't matter that he was old enough to be her grandfather. Between the southern drawl and the wink at the end of his question, this poor girl was smitten. She giggled, nodded and bounced off to get our drinks. It was adorable.

"Now, did Ken ever tell you about the time we had elephants building our camps for us?"

"No, sir."

"He hasn't? Well let me tell you something." And with that James was off and running. I heard stories of basic training and drill sergeants that would have scared R. Lee Ermey. I heard about the jungles of Vietnam and the bouts of food poisoning. I heard about James meeting his wife in a military hospital after getting shot in the arm. How she played hard to get, but James knew he could wear her down eventually. During some of the stories, Ken would raise an eyebrow or shake his head, and James would start on a different wild tale. Apparently, there were parts of the war Ken didn't think I needed to hear about. It was sweet the way he tried to protect me from anything that seemed too horrific, as if I wouldn't be able to handle it. Or maybe he simply thought it wasn't something a girl should hear.

On the ride home, I leaned in between the two seats like a kid, listening to the two of them trade good-humored insults and inside jokes. It was like a lullaby, the soothing sounds of their voices. I leaned back and closed my eyes. I must have drifted off because the next thing I felt was the bump of the car pulling into the driveway and heard them discussing how to wake me up.

"No, don't touch her, James. It scares her. Just whisper her name until she wakes up. She... she gets scared in her sleep. I think she has nightmares." I tried to keep my eyes closed so I could hear what else they would say.

"You still havin' yours?"

"Sometimes. They've gotten better since she came along. Damn near took her arm off the other night though when she tried to wake me up. You should have seen her, James. Looked like I was about to beat her. The worst part is she looked like she thought she may deserve it. You have to promise me something."

"Anything, my friend. You know that."

"You don't ever let that son of a bitch near her again. If you have to kill him, I expect you to do it. That's an order, Corporal, understood?"

"Yes, sir."

"Thank you."

It was time for me to feign waking up. I couldn't take anymore. "Hey, are we home?" I stretched and yawned, pretending I had heard nothing.

"Yes, we are, sleepyhead," Ken answered. "I think we're all ready for a little shut eye."

As we walked into the house, Ken asked if I would mind letting James have my room for the next couple of nights and going back to the recliner. James tried to argue he didn't want to kick me out of my bed, and he was just as capable of sleeping in the living room. I put my foot down.

"Ken, I think this young lady has a little Marine in her. You know, darlin', Marines aren't stubborn. They're just resolved."

I raised my eyebrow. "And some are more resolved than others, sir." They both laughed.

"Sleep tight, kiddo." Ken kissed my forehead on his way out of the living room. James lingered. When we heard the bedroom door shut, he sat down in the rocking chair.

"Persephone, I just wanted to say thank you. I never dreamed dialin' a wrong number would lead to this. You've taken real good care of my friend. I don't think he would have made it this long if it weren't for you." If I was ever going to find out, now was the time. I had to make a decision. Did I want to know, once and for all, what was wrong with Ken? I thought maybe I was finally ready for it.

"James, what's wrong with him? Why is he taking all of those medications?"

"Well now, I figured maybe you and him had talked about this already. But then again, I'm not surprised you haven't. He doesn't like to talk about it. He has acute myeloid leukemia. The treatments stopped working a while ago. He stopped the transfusions and chemo. Said he would rather spend the rest of his life somewhere other than in the hospital or in the bathroom throwin' up."

The next question was so obvious and so hard to ask. I think James could see me struggling to make it come out.

"Not long, darlin'. We just have to hope and pray. It's all we can do. And take care of each other. I don't know that he was supposed to be here this long. That's what I meant when I said you saved him."

"No, James. He saved me. I didn't do anything."

"You may not see it now, Persephone, but you did. He hated himself for not being here when Rachel died. There was nothing he could have done to stop it. It was a car accident. But he still thinks, somehow, if he hadn't enlisted, it wouldn't have happened. You helped him make it up to her. He has finally started forgiving himself. He loves you, Persephone. If he had ever had a daughter, he would have wanted one just like you."

I shook my head. "No he wouldn't. You don't know, James, you don't know who I really am. I'm nothing."

"Look at me, young lady." His voice was full of anger. "Don't you *ever* say that again. I do know you because Ken knows you. Do you have any idea how often he talks about you?"

I hung my head. If they talked that much, that meant James knew everything. The cutting, my parents, everything.

"Persephone?" I shook my head. There was no way I could look him in the eye. "Persephone." It was no longer a question. It was the command of a United States Marine, and there was no way to disobey. I raised my head.

"You know, the one story I didn't tell you tonight was how I got discharged from the Marines. I was shot. Two inches to the left, and it would've hit my heart. Here, let me show you something." He pulled down the neck of his shirt and revealed a puckered scar the size of a half dollar.

"Oh James." Two inches to the left, and he wouldn't be sitting in the living room with me. My breath caught at the possibility.

"I planned to retire as a Marine. That's all I ever wanted to be. But the wound got infected, and even though the bullet missed my heart, the infection didn't. They said I was honorably discharged. I hated everything and everyone for a long time. But, in time, it healed, and the pain started to fade. The scar will always be there. It will always be a part of me, but it's not who I am. Wounds can heal with time, Persephone. And those scars are only a small part of who you can be. Do you understand?"

I nodded.

"You are a strong, intelligent young woman who has fought more battles than most people will ever face in their lifetime. You are going to heal. Ken loves you very much, and so do I. Do you hear me?"

I nodded again.

"No, I asked you a question. Do you hear me?"

"Yes, sir."

"That's better. Now, we're both going to get a good night's sleep."

"Yes, sir."

"Good night, sweet pea."

"Good night."

I was a while going to sleep. The things James had said battled against the things I knew in my heart to be true. The things I learned from the moment I was born. I served one purpose and one purpose only. I was worthless. I was a coward. I was dirty. I was scarred and broken.

No, you're not. You are wounded, but you will heal. And people love you. Love you, without any conditions. They just love you.

My little voice was back, and it was talking fast and furious. I wanted it to shut up. I didn't want to hear it. It hurt. It was terrifying. I couldn't take any more. I didn't want to think. I didn't want to feel. I only wanted to sleep. And right before my brain turned off for the night, the little voice whispered, *we really do love you, sweet pea.*

20.

Graduation day dawned clear and bright. It was almost as if the powers that be took an active interest in the weather, painting the sky a brilliant blue, handcrafting perfectly puffed clouds, and drawing an intense yellow sun only rivaled by that in a child's drawing.

James made breakfast, kept me on track and focus. I got distracted by the piano, text messages from Maggie, birds—basically I was a Chihuahua on crack cocaine. James alternated between laughing and scolding, and waiting on Ken. He seemed worn out from the night before, and we agreed staying in bed until it was time to leave for the ceremony was his best choice.

We didn't talk again about Ken's health. I don't think he had told Ken that I knew, and I didn't say anything either. Now that it was out there, the words were spoken and couldn't be taken back, it was almost as if the worst had already happened. Like James said, there was nothing we could do but hope.

"Persephone! Maggie's reception starts in fifteen minutes! Close the piano!" James bellowed from the kitchen.

"I like listening to her play! She has time to finish!" Ken bellowed from the bedroom, followed by a coughing fit that brought both of us to his door.

"I'm fine, I'm fine. Go back and get me some juice. And Persephone, finish the song. It's one of my favorites." I looked at James and shrugged. *Who knew Ken was a Leonard Cohen fan?* James shrugged back.

"Are you sure you're okay, buddy?"

"Yes, go, please."

We both slowly backed out of the room, looking over our shoulders for a last check as we walked away. Ken waved us on.

"Go finish the song, sweet pea. Maggie will understand if you're a few minutes late. I'll get him some juice."

"Okay."

I started 'Hallelujah' from the beginning and then played 'Everybody Knows' for good measure. Ken was dozing by the time I was done and James was in the living room working on a crossword puzzle.

"I'm going to run on over to Maggie's for a while. I'll be back in about an hour then we can head over to campus." Graduations were held at the massive arena on the college campus because the school gyms were too small to handle the graduates, much less the crowds of friends and family. Parking was a nightmare.

"Sounds good. Drive carefully. See you in a bit."

"Bye, James."

"Bye, sweet pea."

Just as I suspected, Maggie's street was full of Lexuses, BMWs, and Escalades when I pulled up, which meant the house was full of her mom's friends and colleagues. I could only imagine the hell Maggie was experiencing. Or that I was about to. There was no way I was walking in there by myself.

I shot her a text. "Dude! I'm here! Come out and get me!"

A few minutes later, Maggie came flying out the front door, a frantic expression on her face. She started talking before the door had closed behind her.

"I'm so sorry! I didn't know she invited her! She just got here! Persephone, please don't leave! I know you don't want to see her, but please! I need you!"

"Whoa, what are you talking about? Invited who? Who's here?" I grabbed Maggie by the shoulders trying to get her to slow down and make some sense.

"Persephone, your mom is here. And I think she's drunk. She was drunk when she got here, and now she and Mom are talking and drinking wine and it's embarrassing! They're so loud! Please, Persephone!"

Why, God? Why today? Why can't I just have this one *day?*

Maggie kept tugging at my sleeve, pulling me towards the door.

"Maggie, let go. I'm coming. We'll take care of this." I pushed past her and shoved my way into the house. There were people everywhere, the formal living room, the foyer, the kitchen but it was the laughter, the too loud, desperate laughter of the drunk coming from the dining room that concerned me.

I saw her standing by the little table Maggie's mom had set up as a bar, gesturing and talking, spilling wine over the side of her glass as she did. Maggie's mom was cackling at whatever story Mom was telling. *Enough. I have had enough.*

I grabbed her arm from behind. "Mother!"

"Persephone!" Everyone in the room turned at the sound of her screeching my name. "Honey! I was just asking Maggie when you would get here! And then I was telling Darla that I was so disappointed I didn't get to do something like this for you, but you're just not into this kind of thing! Remember when I tried to throw you a birthday party when you were five and you spent the whole time in your room?" *Yes, Mother, because even then I knew enough to know a mom shouldn't be drunk at two in the afternoon.* "Darla, I had all of her little friends over, rented these little bouncy things, had a caterer, the whole nine yards!"

"Mother! Stop shouting!"

"Oh, Persephone, lighten up!" Maggie's mom chastised me. "Your mom is just having fun. Us moms are just trying not to get too sad that our babies are leaving us! Martin! You're here!" Maggie's mom waved wildly at a man across the room. I looked at Maggie in time to catch the expression of horror on her face. I was caught between reining my mother in and figuring out what in the hell was wrong with my friend. I opted for the friend.

"Oh my God, Persephone. She met him at a bar last weekend. And he's. At. My. Graduation. Party!"

"Maggie, it's okay. Come with me. We're leaving."

"It's my graduation party. I can't just leave!"

"Why not? Do you know anyone here? Do you *like* anyone here?"

"Welllll…"

"Exactly. Come on. We'll go hang out with Ken and James. You haven't gotten a chance to meet James yet. We'll get some food and you can ride with us over to graduation. Text your mom later. Come on."

"You know? You're right. Let's go. Wait, my robe and cap. They're up in my room."

While I was waiting for her to get her things, Mom found me again.

"Persephone! Where have you been? You haven't been home in ages! Your dad and I have been worried sick about you!"

"Mom, please, lower your voice," I hissed.

"Don't talk to me like that. How dare you? You know you are still a child, right? You are still my child, and I will not stand for this sort of behavior!" The room was growing quieter, people taking much more interest in whatever was going on between us than their own conversations.

"Mother! Please!"

"No, Persephone! I will not! This is inexcusable! I don't care how grown up you think you are, I will not be treated like this! Like someone you can ignore and leave and throw away! I am your mother for God's sake!"

I looked past her shoulder to see Maggie standing in the doorway. Her face was a mix of horror, embarrassment, and sympathy. She moved forward, and I motioned her to stay back.

"You have to stop this. This is not our home. This is Maggie's party, and you're—"

"You're damn right this isn't our home! You left our home, didn't you? Left me alone!" She began to cry. Mom was not a pretty crier. Her make-up ran and her shoulders hitched. She gulped for air.

"Ladies, maybe you would be more comfortable discussing this outside?"

The man Maggie's mom had invited from the bar was at my elbow. I turned on him. "What the fuck do you think I'm trying to do?"

"Listen, little lady, no one talks to me like that." He grabbed my arm.

"Don't you touch my daughter! No one touches my daughter!" The irony of her statement was not lost on me as she drew back her hand to slap him. She missed and went tumbling to the floor, her wine glass shattering beside her.

"Oh my God! Can you believe this?" I couldn't tell who'd said it, just as I couldn't tell where the laughing began. All I knew was that I had to get her out of there.

"Come on, Mom. Let's go. I'll take you home." I pulled her from the floor, and put my arm around her. Guiding her towards the door, I passed Maggie.

"I'm so sorry, Maggie."

"It's okay, Persephone. Really. I'll see you at the Q, right? You'll be there for the ceremony?"

"Yeah, I'll be there. Just save my place in line, okay?"

"Absolutely. Just put her to bed and hurry over."

"Yep."

Maggie tried to hug me as I walked away. I leaned my head on her shoulder, almost losing my grip on my mom in the process. It seemed Maggie would never stop being a victim of my life.

The drive home was quick, but Mom passed out before we got there anyway. I half-carried, half-walked her into the house. She had forgotten to lock the front door.

"I'm glad you're home, Persephone. This is where you belong," she mumbled as I dropped her on the bed. "Your present is on the table."

"Thanks, Mom." I took off her shoes and covered her with the afghan that was at the end of the bed. She was snoring softly before I shut the door.

I wandered into the kitchen. There was a huge bag with "Congrats Graduate!" and balloons printed all over it. Brightly colored tissue paper spilled out the top. I was too exhausted to even look inside. What could she possibly give me that would matter now?

My phone rang.

"Hello?"

"Well, yes, ma'am, I was hopin' to talk to Ken Austin, please."

"James."

"You comin' home soon, sweet pea? We need to head over soon."

"Yeah, I'm on my way. I just had to drop something off real quick. You guys ready?"

"Absolutely. Havin' fun at Maggie's?"

"Yeah. Lots of people. I'm heading home in just a minute. Just wrapping something up."

"Okay, then. See you soon."

"Yep."

I found a notebook and pen in one of the junk drawers and sat down. How do you say goodbye to your mom? What do you say? I decided to keep it simple.

I love you. Bye, Mom.

It would have to be enough.

21.

Ken and James were waiting in the living room when I got home. They were both dressed in gray suits and dark ties.

"You guys look so handsome!"

"Well, your girl only graduates from high school once." James gave me a hug. Ken remained sitting but held my hand.

"You ready?"

"Yep. Let me grab my cap and gown, and we can go. Who's driving?"

"I thought I would. You've been as jumpy as a toad in a fly swarm today." *Well there's a new one.*

"Fair enough. Ken, are you sure you're up for this?"

"Wouldn't miss it for the world, kiddo. Now let's get going."

James helped him out the chair and followed close behind him on the way to the car. Ken seemed steady on his feet, but he also winced with each step.

"Hey, why don't I drop you two off at the front door when we get there? I'm guessing parking is going to be hard to come by."

"Yeah, that sounds good. Ken, I can show you where to sit and then James can find you, okay?" We both knew Ken wouldn't be able to make it from wherever James ended up parking into the arena. I was concerned about him making it from the front door.

"That sounds fine."

It was a madhouse. There was a line of cars out front with the same idea we had. Cars honking, full of kids yelling at each other, cars full of parents yelling but for different reasons, people crossing the street in herds with no regard for crosswalks or vehicles. I almost had a panic attack just watching.

"Alright, out ya go. I'll be there in two shakes of a lamb's tail."

I held out my arm for Ken to hold onto. He leaned on me more than he had in the past few days, and his breathing seemed to get more labored simply getting out of the car. I told myself it was my imagination. He was still up and around. He was fine.

"You don't have to babysit me, Persephone. Go be with your friends. I can find a place to sit on my own."

"You are my friend. And I'm fine. I want to make sure you get down in front so I can hear you yell when they call my name."

"You bet."

A few classmates caught us on the way in, laughing and chatting. Everyone was friends today, no matter what high school politics had dictated for the past four years. One of them asked if Ken was my grandpa. I smiled, and we kept walking.

I found him a place in the first couple of rows, as promised. I didn't want him climbing steps or walking too far.

"I have to go into the holding area. Are you going to be okay? Do you want me to wait for James to get in here?"

"No, you go. I'm fine."

"If you're sure…"

"I'm sure! Stop hovering and get going!"

"Yes, sir."

There were so many people in the large hallway where we were supposed to meet, I was afraid I would never find Maggie. We had been talking about walking together since we became friends. I couldn't not find her.

"Persephone! Over here!" I saw a small hand reach above the crowd, followed by the top of her bleach-blonde head bouncing up and down as she jumped, trying to get my attention. I pushed my way over to her.

"Here, let me put your cap on for you. Everything okay?"

"Uh, yeah. I put Mom to bed. I don't think I will see her again today. I'm really sorry, Maggie. That was so horrible. I don't know how I can ever make that up to you."

"Hey, it's no biggie. It will be a great story to tell when we're fifty!" She grinned, and I knew she didn't blame me. I wanted to hug her but felt awkward with so many people around.

A teacher started talking over a bullhorn, giving us last minute instructions. We were to write our names on the little cards they handed to us, then give them to the announcer when it was time for us to walk across the stage. And no funny business writing a celebrity's name or bad words. Punishment would be severe. We all looked at each other with the who-me expression teenagers are notorious for. The thought had never even crossed our minds. Riiiight.

We lined up and walked out. The arena erupted from the time the first kid walked out until the last teacher brought up the end. We listened to the welcome and sang the National Anthem. We sat. We listened to speeches no one would remember two weeks later. We listened to another song performed by the honor band. We listened to the principal ask that cheering and clapping be kept brief and polite for each graduate. Then it was time.

Row by row the graduating class was called up. We clapped for the kids we knew, whistled for the ones we deemed more than tolerable. Then it was our row. Maggie and I held hands. They called her name and I screamed myself hoarse. They called my name. Over the brief and polite clapping, I heard two very distinct voices yell, "Oorah!" It was all the cheering I needed.

The last name was called and hats flew. I grabbed one randomly out of the air as they came back down. Pomp and Circumstance began to play, and we filed back out. There was hugging and crying in the holding area, as if we wouldn't be seeing each other again in a few hours. And then it was over. Just like that.

I found Ken and James in the seats where I had left Ken. They were grinning from ear to ear, waiting to sweep me into a hug.

"You did it! We are so proud of you!"

"I did! And I didn't even trip going up the stairs!"

"So, do you want to go somewhere and celebrate?" I looked at Ken, who had sat back down, before answering James' question.

"Uh, no. I think I need a nap if I'm going to be in any shape to make it through Project Graduation tonight. We could maybe grab a pizza on the way home?"

"Sounds like a plan. Why don't you two take it slow, and I'll run out to get the car?"

"Cool." I sat down in the empty seat next to Ken as James walked away.

"I was going to wait until later to give this to you, but now seems like as good a time as any." Ken pulled a small velvet box out of his jacket pocket. Inside was a cameo necklace set in silver. "It belonged to my sister. I sent it to her on her sixteenth birthday. I would like you to have it."

"Oh, Ken. It's beautiful. Thank you." I gently took it out of the box and fastened it around my neck.

"She was a lot like you. Full of life and spirit. And tough. I used to tell her she was a Marine by proxy. A badass in training. I miss her every single day."

I didn't know what to say, so I held his hand. People walked by, some smiled at the sweet picture I'm sure we made. Some said hello. Some didn't even notice us.

"Well, we should probably go see if the grunt has brought the car around."

"Sure." We walked out arm in arm in time to see James pull up to the curb. Ken was asleep before we got home.

22.

Two hours before I was supposed to pick up Maggie and head to the school, James woke me from my nap.

"Persephone, sweet pea, I need you to get up now."

"What time is it?" I looked at my phone. "Not yet," I mumbled rolling back over. "Thirty more minutes."

"It's Ken. We need to take him—"

I was sitting up and pulling on my sneakers before he'd finished the sentence.

"What's wrong with him? Where is he? Should we call an ambulance?"

"No, he doesn't want any of that. We need to go."

Ken was sitting in his recliner, struggling to breathe. His face was a nasty gray color. He didn't look up when I walked in.

"Ken, let's go. Let me help you." *Let me make you better. Please, God, anything.*

James and I got either side of him, and lifted him the best we could. It was a struggle to get him to the car and tucked in the back seat, but somehow we managed. The drive to the hospital was the longest of my life.

At the ER they loaded him onto a gurney and wheeled him away as James answered the admitting nurse's questions. I could do nothing but stare at the door where they had taken my friend. For the second time that day, I silently begged *Please God. Please,* over and over.

There were practical things that needed to be done while we waited for news. I had to call Maggie and tell her I wouldn't be coming to get her. She offered to come sit at the hospital with me. I told her that was ridiculous and to go enjoy her night. Thirty minutes later she texted to say she had decided to hang out with Mick, call if I needed anything. I sent her a smiley face back.

I thought about calling Mom but decided against it. James talked about going back to the house to get whatever paperwork Ken might need. He used nasty words like power of attorney and advanced directive. I tried not to hate him for it.

Frantic parents came in with coughing, feverish children. Cops brought in someone handcuffed and bleeding from a cut above his eye. A woman threw a fit at the front counter because her precious snowflake's stomach hurt, and they had been waiting for almost forty-five minutes. Her son looked ten or so and was sucking his thumb while jabbing the screen of an iPad. He didn't seem nearly as concerned about his tummy ache as his mommy did. James and I waited.

I thought about my mom. Was she awake yet? Once she was back among the living, would she reach for the nearest bottle and go right back under? What would Dad do when he got home? He had found me once, would he find me again? Without Ken, would I have any choice but to go back to his house?

It seemed over the past few weeks, my scars had started to fade. Maybe they hadn't, maybe they just seemed less noticeable. And I hadn't added any new ones in a while. Maybe that helped the healing process, too. I wondered how I would explain them in the years to come. It struck me that I was actually considering years to come. When had that happened?

Maggie sent a text to check on me around ten. I told her we were still sitting in the waiting room. James and I were waiting. Maggie. The friend who never shared her own pain because she was too busy shouldering mine. Even when the weight was almost unbearable. She deserved a sainthood, or at least a medal. I promised myself I would never take her for granted again. I would never lie to someone who tried to love me.

"I'm going to get a cup of coffee. Do you want anything?" James asked.

"No, I'm good. Wait, yeah. Coffee sounds good."

"Anything in it?"

"Nope. The stronger the better."

"Good girl."

I pulled my feet up in the chair and rested my chin on my knees. I had worried for so long who I would be without the scars and the cutting. I worried if I wasn't damaged, enraged, terrified Persephone would there be anything left? My nails were chewed to the quick. I needed to stop doing that.

There was a hole starting to wear in the knee of my jeans. I picked at it. Jeans. I would have to buy my own jeans, with my own money. Money I didn't have. I was used to going shopping for myself, but I typically had cash from Mom in my wallet. And shampoo. And soap. And milk. Memory Lane chocolate milk wasn't cheap, but it was my favorite. And gas. What about my car insurance? The ID cards appeared every six months. I wasn't even sure which company insured me. What the hell was I going to do?

Slow down, kiddo. It doesn't all have to be decided tonight. People do this all the time.

Sure people did, but not this people. This people was scared shitless.

A cup of coffee hovered in front of my face. "Hey, sweet pea, keep your chin up. The doctor will be out soon. I'm sure of it."

"I know. I just…"

James sat down and put his arm around my shoulders. We sat there for a while, sipping the hot coffee-flavored water.

"Ken Austin's family?" The voice was shrill and impatient, as if she had been calling us for hours. They needed to find someone else for that job.

"I guess that's us. Let me talk, okay?"

The woman at the admitting desk waved us through the big, metal double doors. "The doctor will meet you in that waiting room to your left, just through the doors." More waiting.

Surprisingly, she was sitting in a chair waiting for us.

"Are you family?"

"Yes. I hold Ken's power of attorney. This is his granddaughter." *Oh yeah, immediate family only. So I'm not the only one who can lie. Nice.*

"Good. Okay. So, here's the thing. As you both probably know, Ken stopped treatment some time ago. What we're seeing now are the last stages of AML. We're moving him up to ICU now that we have everything stabilized. You will be able to see him in about thirty minutes or so. His oncologist will be in tomorrow morning to talk about more options with you. Are there any questions I can answer for you?" She hit a nice note in tone between: I have twelve other patients backed up behind you guys to take care of, and I really do care and want to help.

James answered for the both of us. "No, I think we're fine. I guess we should just head on up to ICU then?"

"Absolutely. I'll call up and let them know you're coming. Hang out in the waiting room up there and they'll come out and get you when he's ready for visitors. Do you know where it is?" We both shook our heads. "Okay, so you'll go out to the elevators down the hall to your right. Take those up to the fifth floor and then hang a left. The ICU waiting room is right there. You guys take care, okay?"

She grabbed her clipboard, wrapped her stethoscope back around her neck and was gone.

"Well, let's go on up then."

"Yep."

The elevator was empty. It was after visiting hours and most of the nurses were working quietly at their stations. We found the ICU without any problems. There was a middle-aged woman snoozing across two chairs at the far end and the lights were turned down low. James and I waited.

He got up and paced in a little circle. I tapped random buttons on my phone. There weren't any games I wanted to play and no one to call or text. James sat down. The woman made a noise in her sleep and startled herself awake. She rubbed her eyes and looked around.

"Oh gosh, I'm sorry. I wasn't snoring, was I?"

"No, you're fine. It's important to get your rest." James, ever the southern gentleman.

"I've been trying. When she rests I do. At least I try. But my mind, it just goes so many different directions. And it seems like just about the time I drift off, she gets up. Just like when she was a baby." I was afraid I knew who *she* was, and I didn't want to know anymore. "I mean, she never slept, it seemed like. But she never cried, you know? She just wanted to play and snuggle. And sing. It seemed like she was born singing. I want to hear her sing again, you know?"

There weren't any tears. This was a woman who had cried too many times at a Folgers commercial before she knew there were real reasons to cry. She wasn't wasting any more tears on casual conversations. She was going to need them again very soon. She was saving them for that day.

"You will. She will sing for you again." James again. His voice was soothing and sincere. It could almost give you hope, make you believe in a miracle.

Our waiting room companion didn't buy it either. "You are so sweet to say that. You know, I think I'm going to grab a cup of coffee. If they come looking for me, would you mind telling them I will be right back?"

"Yes, ma'am, of course."

I gathered my strength and finally asked the question I had been thinking since James woke me up hours earlier. "James, he's not going to make it, is he?"

"Persephone, he's a fighter. If anyone—"

"No, don't tell me that. Tell me the truth."

He sighed. "No, sweet pea. Not this time. He did what he needed to do. It's time for him to rest now."

"You mean take care of me, don't you?" I was trying to reopen every wound I could and make new ones. I wanted to hear every sad, painful thing I could wring from James and not break.

"Yes, he wanted to take care of you."

"Where will his funeral be? What does he want?"

James swallowed hard. I was being cruel. This was his friend too. He had cared about Ken for much longer than I had. "At the Veterans' Cemetery. It will be a graveside service."

"What about his things? His house? Who will take care of all of it?" I pictured some stranger pawing through his things, assigning values, throwing things away, passing judgment. Another cut. No tears.

"I will. I've read his will, Persephone. He had it changed a bit ago. I know what to do with everything."

"Will you sell everything?"

"Most of it. There are some items I would like to keep. I'm sure there are some things you would like to have as well."

"Yes. His blanket. The one in the living room." It was the deepest cut yet. I was still unshaken.

"I'm sure he would want you to have it. Persephone, Ken is leaving you his sister's piano."

I was broken.

We finally got to go back to see Ken over an hour later. The woman had returned from getting coffee and had gone to see her own patient.

He wasn't awake when the doctor drew back the curtain to his little corner of the ICU. His mouth was covered with an oxygen mask. There were tubes everywhere.

I sat down in the chair next to his bed and took his hand.

"Ken? I don't know if you can hear me."

"He can, sweet pea. Tell him what you need to say."

I need to tell him thank you. I need to tell him I wouldn't have lived this long without him. I need to tell him that he can't go. I can't do this alone. I need to tell him I'm scared. I need to tell him I wouldn't know who John Irving was if it weren't for him. I need to tell him...

"Ken, it's Persephone. I love you."

James and I waited. I sat, holding Ken's hand, and James stood behind me. A nurse came by and looked at all the machines. She made a note in Ken's chart and moved on to the next bed.

James moved to the other side. He laid his hand on Ken's shoulder.

"Your tour is almost over, old friend. You can go home." The steady beat of the heartrate monitor continued. "Persephone, you need to let him go."

"No. I want my friend. Please, James. Please give me back my friend." I was using the only words I could find. Words I stole from Ken's favorite author.

"Sweet pea, he will always be with you."

"Ken..." I looked up at James. "I can't do it. I just can't."

"Yes, you can, darlin'. He won't go until he knows you're okay."

I wanted to be selfish. I wanted to stay by that bed, holding his hand. I wanted the world to stop. I wanted to hear him call me a pup again, tell me what page we left off on, and that he loved me. But most of all, I wanted his pain to be over.

"Thank you, Ken. I love you. It's okay."

It felt like his fingers curled around mine and squeezed, if only for a moment. The rhythmic ticks and bleeps stopped. There was only the continuous single bleat from the heart monitor. The nurse came over and turned it off.

She checked his pulse for the sake of formality and patted my arm. "I am so sorry, honey. Please take your time."

I looked at James. This wasn't it, was it? He wasn't really gone? The tears pouring down his face answered my questions.

I couldn't breathe. I couldn't stand. I couldn't feel anything except the hurt. Something was sitting on my chest. Something was clawing at my heart. There was something burrowing through my brain.

"Persephone, he loved you so much." He leaned down and kissed Ken's forehead. "I love you, my friend. You will be missed. You were one of the good ones."

"I can't let go, James. I just can't."

"Yes, you can. Come on, sweet pea. It's going to be okay."

James led me out of the ICU, through the hallways and out to the car. We didn't talk on the way home. The house was empty and awful. It felt like someone had come in and moved everything a few inches off center.

I went to my bedroom as James started a pot of coffee. The piano was waiting for me. I played 'Amazing Grace' and heard James crying in the kitchen. Later, we would comfort each other. Tonight, we wrapped ourselves in grief for our lost friend.

23.

James went to the hospital the next morning to take care of the paperwork and arrangements. It seemed so cold and formal. I pretended to be asleep when he left. I was still lying in bed, staring at the sun coming through the window when I heard the doorbell. I assumed it was Maggie. I had texted her when we got home but told her I didn't feel like talking. I would call her later. I didn't even bother looking out the window before answering the door.

I was unprepared to see my father standing there.

"Well, young lady, I'm assuming you're quite proud of yourself? Little stunt you pulled with your mom? She called me in hysterics last night. I took the red eye in from Alabama. Now you go get your stuff and get your ass in the car." He made a grab for my arm. I pulled away and backed a few steps into the house.

Who was I to stand up to him? *You are the badass in training. The Marine by proxy.*

I didn't have any strength left to fight. *You are wounded, but you will heal.*

I was nothing. *He loved you so much, sweet pea.*

Those voices, they would always be a part of me. No matter where I went, they would go with me. And no matter what enemy I was facing, there would always be two Marines standing guard behind me. "Oorah."

"Excuse me? I told you to move your ass."

"Go to hell." He opened his mouth to say something. "No, shut up and listen. You are a worthless piece of shit. If you ever, *ever* come near me or anyone I care about ever again, I will tell everyone and anyone who will listen exactly who you are and what you do. Do you understand me?"

He laughed. "Honestly, Persephone, who's going to believe—"

"It will only take one, *Dad*. One person who even thinks there's a possibility it might be true and everything is over for you. You don't get to be in control anymore. You don't get to hurt me. Get the hell out of my life. You are nothing to me. Nothing, do you understand?" I was yelling by now, walking towards him, backing him down the driveway.

"Persephone, if you don't get in this car right now, you are never welcome to my home again. Never. You won't get a dime from us. We will no longer have a daughter. Is that what you want?"

It was my turn to laugh. "More than you will ever know."

"Fine. To hell with you then, you little ungrateful bitch."

There were so many things I wanted to say. So many vile, disgusting things I could have hurled at him. But it was enough to see him get in his car and drive away.

Oorah, kiddo, oorah.

EPILOGUE

I never went back to my mother and father's house. James stayed with me at Ken's until it was time for me to leave for college. Together, we loaded my small car and the back of his truck with clothes and dorm furnishings. There were students there to help me carry everything to my room, so he didn't have to. We said our goodbyes in the parking lot.

"Ken would have been so proud of you."

I tried hard not to cry but didn't succeed.

I graduated with my degree in counseling and immediately found a job at a crisis center two blocks from the apartment I lived in alone. It was there I met Adam. After our third date, I told him everything—why there were scars all over my body, why he would most likely never meet my parents, and, most importantly, about Ken. Adam didn't say a word while I talked. He held my hand and listened.

Finally, when I took a breath, he gently turned my wrist over and kissed the scars there. "I know I can't heal these, but can I help you try?"

We were married six months later at a small bed and breakfast in Eureka Springs. It wasn't fancy, but neither were we. James stood by my side, and when the minister asked who gives this woman, he answered, "I do."

Adam and I put off going to Springfield as long as we could, claiming busy schedules and clients who needed us. I didn't feel particularly bad about this. Mom could have driven south just as easily.

A few months before our two-year anniversary, Mom called, hysterical. Dad was in the hospital, massive heart attack. I didn't want to go. There was nothing I could do. Nothing I wanted to do. It took Adam close to three hours to convince me I needed, for my own sake, to go say goodbye. It was the first time we had ever fought.

We packed our overnight bags and got on the road. He died before we got there. I would like to say I cried, but I didn't.

Three years later, our son was born. Austin James. His favorite blanket is an old Marine Corps fleece that still smells like vanilla and sandalwood.

THANK YOU

First and foremost I want to thank my family. My amazing husband and daughter, Dana and Hannah, who supported and believed in me every step of the way. You two are my everything, and I love you.

I have two sisters, a brother, two brothers-in-law, a sister-in-law, two nephews, and a niece (Jenn, Tom, Chelsea, Jeff, Kyle, Erin, Brady, TJ, and Harper) all within a fifteen minute drive. The close proximity may drive us all to drink sometimes, but I wouldn't have it any other way. I couldn't have done this without all of you.

And my mom and dad, Charley and Lisa Slavens. You two taught me what being a real hero means. Your love, compassion, and unwavering support mean more than I will ever be able to find words to express.

Thank you to my ever-patient editors, Evangeline Jennings and Lucy Middlemass. They deserve sainthood after putting up with me during this process. If you liked the book, thank them. If you didn't, blame me. It means I didn't take their advice when I should have.

And finally, thank you. Thank you for giving me a little piece of your time and letting me share Persephone's story with you. You are the reason I write.

Layla Harding, June 2015

In 2013, approximately 679,000 children were victims of abuse.

A portion of the proceeds from this book will be donated to The Child Advocacy Center in Springfield, Missouri. For more information, please visit their website at www.childadvocacycenter.org

COMING SOON

FIRST GIRL ON THE MOON

LUCY MIDDLEMASS EVANGELINE JENNINGS

A Young Adult Collection

Brothers and sisters
Fathers and daughters
First loves
Second thoughts

Elizabeth is furious
Felicity isn't happy
Magda's family won't answer the phone
Isobel is smitten
Vivienne is going to fuck her sister's boyfriend
And me—the girl without a name? I'm all about Alex
And Alex is the first girl on the Moon

RIDING IN CARS WITH

GIRLS

EVANGELINE
JENNINGS

starshy

"A smashing, original collection likely to be read again
and again"
Kirkus Reviews

http://getbook.at/Evie

CPSIA information can be obtained
at www.ICGtesting.com
Printed in the USA
LVOW01s1438010216
473175LV00021B/910/P